Louisa pushed back her chair and stood up—her face ashen.

A frown knotted her forehead above the wide, gray eyes. Nervously she pushed back a lock of pale, honey gold hair and secured it with the tortoiseshell comb holding the mass of curls around her shoulders. Her slender build and tiny waist lent an air of frailty.

"Nothing else?" Louisa demanded as she twisted her lace handkerchief into knots. "When is he coming back?"

"I have no idea." Jack Bradford paused and dabbed at his dark mustache with his napkin. "Peter actually ran out of the bank with a wild look on his face. He had an air of mystery about him and didn't want to stop and chat. I must say, Louisa, your fiancé seemed a bit strange today."

"I don't understand, Father!" Louisa exclaimed. "We've just completed all the work at the house, and Peter loved every detail. It's beautiful and ready for us to move into as man and wife. Why would he leave town without telling me his destination? It doesn't make any sense!" Louisa blotted her eyes with her handkerchief and blew her nose.

Elizabeth Bradford stood up and reached to comfort her daughter. "There, there," she soothed as she pulled her only child against her ample bosom. She stooped slightly as she wrapped long, fleshy arms around Louisa. Honey blond hair, somewhat darker than her daughter's, coiled neatly into a bun at the nape of her neck. Her green eyes, although clouded now with concern, bore a mischievous twinkle at times. "Everything will be all right, dear," Mrs. Bradford murmured. "It must be something important. Wait and see."

CAROL MASON PARKER makes her home in northern Michigan. She is a wife and mother of four grown children. Carol's desire is to write novels that "honor and glorify God."

Books by Carol Mason Parker

HEARTSONG PRESENTS
HP104—Haven of Peace
HP231—A Time to Love

Best Laid Plans

Carol Mason Parker

Heartsong Presents

God has blessed my husband Herb and me with four children. This book is dedicated to our wonderful children: Cynthia, Mark, David, and Kimberly; their dear spouses and our precious grandchildren.

I have no greater joy than to hear
that my children walk in truth.
3 JOHN VERSE 4

A note from the author:
I love to hear from my readers! You may correspond with me by writing: **Carol Mason Parker**
Author Relations
PO Box 719
Uhrichsville, OH 44683

ISBN 1-58660-067-2

BEST LAID PLANS

All Scripture quotations are taken from the King James Version of the Bible.

All of the characters and events in this book are fictitious. Any resemblance to actual persons, living or dead, or to actual events is purely coincidental.

Cover illustration by Kathi Tustin.

PRINTED IN THE U.S.A.

one

1868

Louisa Bradford hummed a little tune as she walked quickly along Main Street away from the shops in town. She carried a light package under one arm, and a smile played about her lips as she considered the new frock she had just purchased. It was a mint green satin with delicate lace and tiny buttons. The dress made her feel special, and the saleslady insisted the color was right for her because it accented the gray of her eyes. Louisa gave a little skip as she contemplated how the dress would affect her beau, Peter McClough. They had been seeing one another for some time, but she sensed tonight would be different. Peter seemed rather eager when he mentioned his plans for the evening, and the glint in his eye lent an air of mystery. He had hinted it would be a special occasion, and Louisa felt this particular event warranted a new gown. Excitement mounted within her breast as she thought about Peter. He was tall and muscular, not overly handsome, but with rugged good looks. She loved the way a shock of his dark hair occasionally fell across his forehead. His dark eyes held her attention and gazed deep into her soul. At times he knew what she was thinking and what she was about to say. Their friendship, rocky at first, had grown into a sweet and caring relationship.

It was a warm August afternoon in Waterville, Maine, and Louisa reached up with her free hand and loosened the ribbons on her straw bonnet. A slight breeze toyed with her pale, golden tresses as they cascaded about her shoulders. She hoped her new dress would impress Peter as much as it had her. Anxious to inspect her purchase once again, she hurried down a side street and turned in at the Bradfords' large two-story home. Her banker father would be at work, but she was eager to show her mother the gown and seek her approval.

"Mother, I'm home," she called as she placed her bonnet on a hook and dropped the package on a pine bench by the front door. "Where are you?" Dead silence met her repeated calls and then she remembered. Her mother had a ladies' meeting at church and wouldn't be home until later. "Oh fiddle! I so wanted Mama to see my beautiful gown right away," she muttered aloud. Louisa grabbed the package, untied the string, and held the satiny frock against her body. "It's exquisite!" she exclaimed, as she viewed her image in the mirror over the bench in the entryway. "I must find the appropriate jewelry to go with it—something very special."

Louisa dashed up the stairs and in a very short time stood, dressed in her new gown, before a full-length mirror in her bedroom. She emptied her jewelry box and tried on several neckpieces. "None of these are right with this dress," she moaned. "I should have purchased something new to compliment the gown." She tossed her jewelry back into the case and headed for her parents' bedroom. She was sure her mother would gladly loan her a piece of her jewelry. Elizabeth Bradford had often suggested that her only daughter should wear one of her necklaces or a particular broach for a special occasion. Louisa lifted her mother's case from the top of her dresser and pulled out several pieces of jewelry. She held each piece up to her throat and gazed into the mirror. A deep sigh escaped her lips as she decided nothing seemed suitable. She was about to replace the several items when she noticed a false bottom with a little ribbon pull tab in her mother's jewelry box—something she had never seen before. Usually her mother brought pieces of jewelry to Louisa's room for her to try on. Louisa pulled on the ribbon and found it opened to display a beautiful gold locket nestled in old satin. Excitement mounted within her as she tenderly lifted the lovely piece and held it to her throat. It was the perfect accompaniment to set off her gown. She turned it over in her hands and found the initials *L.A.M.* engraved on the back. When she opened the locket, she found a picture of a lovely young woman. Eagerly she placed the locket around her neck.

"Maybe it's my great-grandmother," she whispered, as she whirled around the room. "It can't be my grandmother's. Her name was Abigail."

Louisa decided to keep the necklace on until her mother returned home, so she could see how beautiful it looked with her new gown. She pulled the satiny cloth out of the box to straighten it and found a faded picture underneath. It was a picture of two young ladies with their arms about each other's waists. "The one on the right is my mother," Louisa said audibly, "when she was about fifteen or sixteen years old." She turned the picture over and found inscribed in her mother's handwriting, "Louisa and I, best of friends, June 1847." Louisa puzzled over the picture and wondered why her mother had never mentioned her dear friend of long ago. Obviously Louisa had been named for this person. Why had her mother never told her? Was there some reason she kept the locket and picture hidden?

When Louisa heard the front door open, she rushed to the top of the stairs with the picture clutched in her hand. "Mother!" she cried. "I'm upstairs. Come up and see my new gown. I hope you will like it. It's beautiful!"

"I'll be right up, dear, as soon as I remove my hat and gloves. I'm sure the dress is lovely. What time is Peter calling for you?"

"About six o'clock. I have plenty of time, so I'll change my gown and help you prepare dinner for you and Father. But you must see my outfit first. And may I wear a piece of your jewelry? I've found just the right neckpiece to give it a perfect touch."

"Of course, dear. You know I like to share my jewelry with you," Elizabeth Bradford said as she climbed the stairs and eyed her daughter's new gown. She leaned over and kissed Louisa's cheek. "You are right; it is indeed beautiful. You have excellent taste. Peter will be overcome."

"And the locket, Mama. I found it at the bottom of your jewelry box hidden underneath. It complements the dress so well. I hope you don't mind if I wear it."

Elizabeth Bradford glanced at the neckpiece for the first time, and her face turned ashen. "Why. . .how. . . ," she stammered.

"The initials, Mama, are *L.A.M.* on the locket. And this picture," Louisa still clutched it and held it out to her mother, "is a picture of you and your very dearest friend, Louisa. Why did you never tell me about her? Is she the one you named me after?"

Elizabeth Bradford grabbed the picture from Louisa's hand and hurried into her room with Louisa right on her heels. "What's wrong, Mother? Didn't you want me to see the picture?"

Tears trickled down Elizabeth Bradford's fair cheeks as she sat down on her bed. For a few moments she was unable to speak. "No, Louisa," she sighed, "I never wanted you to see the locket or the picture. That is why I kept them hidden in the bottom of my jewelry case. I thought they were safe there. . . safe from your eyes. . .safe from questions and answers."

"I'm sorry, Mama," Louisa said as she sat next to her mother on the bed and hugged her close. "I didn't think you would mind. You always want me to wear your jewelry, so I took the liberty of going into your jewelry case. I realize now it was wrong of me. But what is wrong with my seeing these things? Why did you keep them from me?"

Elizabeth Bradford wiped her tears on her lace hanky and blew her nose. "Your father always thought I should tell you, Louisa, but I was afraid to. Afraid it would alienate you from me. Afraid I would lose your love."

"Tell me what, Mother? Is it something so secret that I cannot know?"

"Now there is nothing else to do but to tell you the entire story. I hope you will accept what I have to say and not be angry with me."

"Never, Mother! I love you! I couldn't be angry with you. I'm grown up. I hope I'm mature enough to understand whatever you tell me."

Elizabeth Bradford patted her daughter's hand and spoke softly. "Louisa Ann McKay was my dearest friend. Our families lived near one another in Augusta. We went through grade school together and into the higher classes as soul mates. The two of us were inseparable, always together." Elizabeth hesitated briefly and looked away from her daughter's intense gaze. A deep sigh escaped her lips. "The picture you found was taken when my friend and I were both sixteen—still very close after all those childhood years. When I met your father, we fell in love and not long after were married. Louisa and I were still the best of friends and pledged our friendship to one another. Louisa became pregnant and refused to tell me who the father of her child was. I begged her to tell me, but she was stubborn and would not divulge her secret. The McKays, wealthy people and high on the social roll, insisted she give the baby up for adoption. They wanted nothing to do with the child. Before you were born, Louisa pleaded with me and your father to adopt her child. It was a planned ahead transaction. I wanted to do it for Louisa's sake, although I wondered how difficult it would be for her to know her child's adoptive parents."

Louisa's face turned ashen with shock as she grasped the meaning of her mother's words. "I. . .I am Louisa McKay's child, born out of wedlock?" she asked. "And no one knows who my real father is?"

"No one," Elizabeth answered as she pulled her daughter

close to her breast. "That is one reason I didn't want you to know about this. I couldn't bear to lose your love. You are my daughter—our daughter, your father's and mine—as much as our own flesh and blood would have been. We wanted other children, but it was not in God's plan for us. We love you, Louisa."

"I know, Mama," Louisa sobbed lightly against her mother's breast. "And I couldn't love you and Father any less because of this. You are the parents I've always known and will always love. But what about Louisa McKay? Did she ever marry? Did she want to see me? Did she care about me at all?"

"Louisa died in childbirth, dear, and I was heartbroken. She had always been rather frail, and something went wrong with the birth. It was tragic to lose my dearest friend. She was so young and full of life. But it was a blessing for me to have you, a part of her, to care for and raise as my own. Louisa never got to hold you, or name you, or care for you. I wanted to name you after her, and your father agreed. Louisa Ann Bradford. Only your last name is different. A lovely name for a lovely girl."

"So I have grandparents, the McKays, in Augusta? Didn't they care about me after I was born? Didn't they want to see me?"

"I regret that they did not. The McKays could not bear the embarrassment. They moved out west somewhere after Louisa died and built a new life. It was as if you never existed to them. They were glad your father and I adopted you, but they wanted to be out of the picture entirely. They instructed me to keep everything secret and raise you as my own. That was part of the agreement. It's their loss, Louisa. You are so like your real mother. The McKays will never know the lovely granddaughter they could have shared their life with. And your father and I thought it best to move from Augusta to Waterville. A change of scenery, all new people. No one here knew that you were not our own child by birth."

Elizabeth Bradford held her daughter against her bosom

for several moments as Louisa sobbed quietly. She stroked her daughter's hair and sang a song from Louisa's childhood in her sweet soprano voice. The words had a soothing effect for each of them as they clung to one another and rocked gently back and forth. Several moments passed before Elizabeth Bradford relaxed her grip on her daughter. "We don't want to wrinkle your new gown, dear. This is an important evening for you. Go ahead and wear the locket. It's yours to keep and someday pass on to your own daughter. Your birth mother," Elizabeth choked on her words, "would have been so proud of you."

Louisa straightened her frock, dabbed at her eyes, and stood up. "I feel so strange, Mama. It's like a story being told, but it's not fiction. Instead, it is about me. I'm not sure I can fathom this all at once. Do you have other pictures. . .or memory things from my. . .birth mother? If so, I want to see them. I hope you will understand, but I must see them."

"I understand, dear. And I do have pictures from our early days and high school years. Also a few mementoes in my old scrapbook. I'll show them to you another time." She held up the picture Louisa found with the locket. "This one of my friend and me together was my very favorite. That's why I kept it with the locket."

&

Peter McClough arrived promptly at six, and Louisa descended the staircase in her new gown. She could feel his eyes upon her and hoped no trace of her former tears lingered. Her gown, pressed to perfection, accented the gentle curves of her slender body. The sweetheart neckline of her frock fell just below the lovely gold necklace. Her pale, gold hair, brushed and shining, fell in a mass of curls about her shoulders.

A soft whistle of appreciation escaped Peter's lips, and he reached for her hand. "You are a beautiful vision, Louisa," he said huskily. "I need to touch you to be sure you aren't just a dream."

Louisa's dimpled smile spread across her face as she gazed into his dark eyes. "I'm real, Peter, and very much alive." She reached up and touched his cheek. "I must say you look very handsome, Sir, in your dark suit and striped tie."

Peter took her arm and tucked it into his as he escorted her across the hallway. "I'm taking you to a special place tonight because this is a most important evening. I hope," he said mysteriously, "it will be the best of my whole life."

They called their good-byes to Louisa's parents with promises to be home at an early hour. Mixed emotions filled Louisa's mind as they headed down the road toward Main Street in Peter's carriage. She wondered where he was taking her. They had visited every restaurant in town several times. Why was Peter being so secretive? She loved him and had for a long time—this man with the boyish face and shock of dark, unruly hair. He had never proposed and often said he wanted her to be sure of her feelings before they made a commitment to each other such as marriage. She knew it was due to his background and the kind of life he had led. But God had changed him—changed him from a loud, raucous, self-centered young man into the caring man he was now. It was a change of heart, a change of his former type of life. Peter McClough had repented of his sins and had accepted Jesus Christ as Lord of his life. The change in Peter delighted Louisa, but now she must tell him about her secret— her background, especially if he planned to propose. The news she had so recently learned was too important to keep hidden from the man she loved. Peter must know the details. She was a child born out of wedlock—adopted by the Bradfords. Louisa shuddered slightly as she wondered if her birth news would make a difference to him.

Peter maneuvered the reins with a flip of his wrist on a pair of bay horses and glanced at Louisa. She had pulled a white shawl across her shoulders. "You are very quiet this evening," he teased. "Is anything wrong?"

Louisa leaned her head against his shoulder. "I'm excited, Peter," she said, evading his question. "Where are we going?"

"You'll see soon enough. It's a new place out of town on the old Webb Road. I've heard some good comments about the food. I thought we should try it and see for ourselves."

Shortly thereafter they arrived at a small but quaint restaurant nestled in a grove of pine trees. From the number of carriages tied at the hitching post, Louisa realized it must be a popular spot. They were soon inside and settled at a table set very privately in a back corner away from the eyes of the other clientele. The wall paintings, candles, colorful table cloth, and pink flower centerpiece caught Louisa's eye.

"It's lovely," she sighed, glancing around her. "You are right, Peter. It's a very special place."

"The food will tell the tale. I'd heard this place was decorated nicely, but let's hope the food is as good or better than the rumors I've heard. I'm starved. How about you?"

Louisa studied the menu and fumbled with her napkin. Actually the news she received earlier in the day had ruined her appetite, but she determined to make every effort to disguise her feelings. "I'm anxious to see how delicious the food is, Peter. I'm sure it will be as excellent as the decorations."

As the couple ate their dinners, Louisa tried to form in her mind the right words to tell Peter about her past. Should she just blurt it out or work up to it in some way? She didn't want to spoil the evening, with all its glamour and beauty, too soon. *Maybe after dessert would be a good time. Peter will be fully satisfied with his meal and in a good mood.*

Louisa was not prepared when the waitress brought a small cake and placed it on the table before her. "I understand this is a very special occasion," the waitress said with a smile. "I hope you like the cake. It was special ordered." The white cake had a tiny layer on top, and the waitress cut it out and put it on a plate before Louisa. "Enjoy!" she said with a sly glance at Peter, and walked away.

"Go ahead and eat," Peter said with a grin. "I'll help myself to a larger piece."

"I'm so full, Peter. I'll save it and take it home with me. I can eat it tomorrow. I'll enjoy it more then. The rest of the cake isn't that big. Why don't you eat all of it?"

"No you don't, Louisa!" Peter insisted. "You must eat your piece now, and I'll eat the rest. It's part of our celebration."

"What is the celebration?" Louisa asked as she dug her fork into the piece of cake. But the fork hit something hard and brittle. "Something is wrong with this cake, Peter!" Puzzled, she pushed the cake apart with her fork and exposed a small jewelers' box. "What's this?" she asked, wide-eyed with excitement.

"Open it and see, darling," Peter urged as he handed her his napkin. "Wipe the box off first."

With trembling hands, Louisa wiped the cake from the box and opened it. "Peter!" she cried, as she examined its contents. "It's a ring—a beautiful ring!" She lifted it out and studied the magnificent piece of jewelry. In a gold setting nestled a large diamond surrounded with about eight smaller ones. "I've never seen such a beautiful diamond ring," she said in a hushed tone.

Peter reached across the table and took it from her hand. "I love you, Louisa. Will you marry me, darling? I've waited a long time to ask you this important question. I want to marry you, with God's blessing, and love you forever."

Louisa sat speechless for several moments and then burst into tears.

two

Peter jumped up and moved his chair closer to Louisa. "Darling, I thought you would be happy," he said putting his arm around her. "Why are you crying?"

"I am happy, Peter. I always cry when I'm happy."

"Then you will marry me? Please say yes."

Louisa lifted her face to Peter and smiled through her tears. "Yes, yes, yes! I've waited for this moment for a long time."

Peter slipped the ring on her finger and brushed away her tears. Then he cupped her face in his hands and kissed her— a sweet lingering kiss to seal their words of commitment. " 'Grow old along with me. . .the best is yet to be. . . ,' " he whispered huskily against her hair as he quoted from Robert Browning. "Darling, this is the best day of my life, so far. It will only be better when you are Mrs. Peter McClough."

"Mrs. Peter McClough," she echoed. "It sounds wonderful to me."

"How soon, dearest?" he asked. "How soon can we be married?"

Louisa held up her hand and turned it over and over to see how the diamonds in her ring sparkled. "It takes time to plan a wedding, Peter. I'll have to talk with Mother. She'll want to sew my wedding gown and gowns for my attendants."

"And I must ask your parents for permission, Louisa. Do you think they will consent and trust their only child to me? They've known me for a long time now and have seen the changes in my life. Surely they knew my intentions were serious."

Louisa smiled up at Peter and said softly. "I think they've

wondered if you were ever going to ask me. They know pretty much how I feel about you."

Peter stood up, his face flushed and excited. "Let's go home so I can talk to them. I'll ask for your hand in marriage, and with their permission, we will set the day."

As the horses trotted toward the Bradford home, Louisa listened to the familiar clip-clop of their hooves on the hard, clay road. It was a lovely evening and glistening stars dotted the magnificent heavens. She felt comfortable with just a shawl about her shoulders to ward off the chill in the night air. Although elated over Peter's proposal, her happiness was overshadowed by the news about her birth. She wasn't really a Bradford, after all, and she didn't have any knowledge of her real father. Why did this happen today of all days—to mar such a special occasion? She must tell Peter and get it out in the open. He, of all people, would surely understand.

"Peter," she said clutching his arm, "I have something to tell you about my past, and I want you to listen. It's important to me that you hear the entire story."

Peter guided the horses at a slow gait and headed toward town. "Of course, darling. What is so important about your past that you must confess it now? Have you kept a big, dark secret from me?"

"You may consider this a big, dark secret, Peter, but I only learned about it today by accident. I couldn't have told you or anyone else the circumstances earlier."

Louisa took a deep breath and started. She repeated every detail of the afternoon—her shopping trip, finding the locket and picture in her mother's jewel case, and her mother's dismay when she arrived home. When she related the part about her birth mother, she choked up and could not go on.

Peter reined in the horses and pulled off to the side of the road. He turned to Louisa, drew her close, and held her in his arms. "It's all right, darling. I understand. I'm sorry you had to find out that way. But it doesn't matter. Your folks, the

Bradfords, are your real parents. They've nurtured you, taught you, guided you, and given you so much care all these years. We know they love you as their own, and that is what counts. Don't you agree?"

"Yes, Peter, but do you mind about the fact of my birth? I have no knowledge of my birth father—who he is or where he is. Does this bother you?"

"I love you, Louisa. These incidents could never change that. Besides, you have not been concerned about my past, which was colorful to say the least." Peter flipped the reins and headed the horses back to the roadway. "Let's get on home and talk to your folks. I want their permission to marry the girl who will share my future!"

It was a happy scene at the Bradford home when Peter obtained permission to marry their daughter. A wedding date was set tentatively for mid-October or November to give ample time to sew Louisa's wedding gown and other articles of clothing. The remaining weeks of August found the couple deliriously happy as they courted and planned for the future. They would live in Peter's fine home, the one he had inherited from the widow Maude McClough, his father's second wife. Peter gave Louisa free rein to replace a few pieces of furniture in the large home, and she and her mother sewed new curtains for each of the rooms. By mid September the house was completely redone to suit her taste and met with Peter's approval. The couple discussed several fall wedding dates, but a definite date had not been established.

≈

"Peter McClough left town this afternoon," Jack Bradford announced to his wife and daughter as they sat at the dinner table one September evening. "I saw him at my bank this morning, and he said he was leaving on the one o'clock train."

The trio sat around the walnut dining table in their large brick home. Jack Bradford, a banker, was a tall man of medium build with dark hair and eyes. His spectacles sat low on his nose as he studied his daughter's reaction.

"Why, Father?" Louisa gasped, as she dropped her fork with a loud clatter on her delicate china plate. "Where is he going?"

"Didn't say," Mr. Bradford said and helped himself to another slice of ham. "Peter seemed distracted and appeared to be in a great hurry. He didn't stop to talk, but said to tell you 'good-bye.'"

Louisa pushed back her chair and stood up—her face ashen. A frown knotted her forehead above the wide, gray eyes. Nervously she pushed back a lock of pale, honey gold hair and secured it with the tortoiseshell comb holding the mass of curls around her shoulders. Her slender build and tiny waist lent an air of frailty.

"Nothing else?" Louisa demanded as she twisted her lace handkerchief into knots. "When is he coming back?"

"I have no idea." Jack Bradford paused and dabbed at his dark mustache with his napkin. "Peter actually ran out of the bank with a wild look on his face. He had an air of mystery about him and didn't want to stop and chat. I must say, Louisa, your fiancé seemed a bit strange today."

"I don't understand, Father!" Louisa exclaimed. "We've just completed all the work at the house, and Peter loved every detail. It's beautiful and ready for us to move into as man and wife. Why would he leave town without telling me his destination? It doesn't make any sense!" Louisa blotted her eyes with her handkerchief and blew her nose.

Elizabeth Bradford stood up and reached to comfort her daughter. "There, there," she soothed as she pulled her only child against her ample bosom. She stooped slightly as she wrapped long, fleshy arms around Louisa. Honey blond hair, somewhat darker than her daughter's, coiled neatly into a bun at the nape of her neck. Her green eyes, although clouded now with concern, bore a mischievous twinkle at times. "Everything will be all right, dear," Mrs. Bradford murmured. "It must be something important. Wait and see."

Louisa welcomed the comfort of the large arms wrapped around her for a few moments. The soft plumpness of her mother's body proved a soothing escape from the news of Peter's departure. Suddenly she jerked away. "Men! I'll never understand them! One moment Peter talks of our wedding day, and the next moment, he is off somewhere on a trip. Why are men so difficult?"

Elizabeth Bradford smiled slightly as she glanced at her husband. "I know you are upset with Peter, Louisa, but aren't you judging him prematurely? And I don't think we can consider all men the same or bunch them together. Many men, like your father, are steady and dependable. I'm sure you will find Peter is, also."

"Of course, Father," Louisa said running to him. "I didn't mean you." She planted a kiss on his cheek, knocking his spectacles awry. "It's men like Peter. He's so unpredictable. One minute he cares about me, and the next minute, he's off somewhere."

Jack Bradford cleared his throat and adjusted his spectacles, which had a tendency to slip down on his nose. "I admit Peter seemed in a big rush and not willing to talk, but let's give him the benefit of the doubt. He's been going to Colby College and using his father's money that he inherited wisely. Perhaps he's checking out another college somewhere. Isn't that a possibility?"

"It could be another college, Father, but why didn't he share his plans with me? After all, we are engaged to be married. And surely he would have talked about another school if that were a possibility. We've spent so much time together lately redoing the house and picking out fabrics. He's never mentioned going away—for any reason. In fact, it sounds like an unstable thing to do. I wonder if Peter has changed his mind about getting married. Perhaps he is having second thoughts about his freedom and doesn't want to be tied down."

"Why don't you finish your dinner, dear? Elizabeth Bradford suggested. "You're making too much out of this. Perhaps it's school as your father suggested. Or it could be another job somewhere with challenging possibilities. Wherever he is, he probably has you foremost in his thoughts. If I ever saw a man in love, it's Peter McClough!"

"All my friends are married," Louisa moaned. "My dearest friend, Emily Mason, is now Mrs. Robert Harris. Wasn't it a strange coincidence when we found out Emily's Uncle George was Peter's father? So she and Peter are cousins."

"Peter served at the same army base as Frederic, Emily's brother, didn't he?" Jack Bradford asked. "They were actually war buddies and didn't realize they were cousins."

"According to Peter, they were together for a short time during the war. But Peter despised Frederic because of his Christian stand. He swore at him, called him a goody-goody, and tried to pick fights with him. Peter regrets his actions, and he and Fred are close friends now." Louisa paused, her brow furrowed. "I wish Peter were more predictable."

"Peter changed for the good, Louisa," her mother said, "and we've all noticed the difference. I believe you are just overanxious, dear. Have a little patience."

Louisa sighed audibly. "I haven't heard a word from Emily since she and Robert married three months ago. I hope I get a letter soon, so I'll have her complete address. I'm sure she'll have a lot to tell me about her life as a pastor's wife in Pennsylvania."

"You'll need to let her know as soon as your wedding date is finalized," Elizabeth Bradford said. "Does she know about your engagement?"

"I sent word to her through her parents, so I should be hearing back soon. She will be happy for us, but now maybe there won't be a wedding. Peter is off somewhere, and I don't have the slightest idea where he's gone. Perhaps I'll end up an old maid, Mother."

Jack Bradford choked on his coffee and sputtered, "You're not an old maid, Louisa, so don't act like one. Peter will probably be back by the end of the week."

Louisa twisted her napkin and glanced at her mother. "I'm twenty years old and not married yet. How old were you when you and Father married, Mother?"

"You are not an old maid, Louisa," her mother insisted. "Twenty years of age doesn't make you an old maid. Be a little patient with Peter. He's the one who has been anxious to consummate this marriage. Something evidently came up, and he needed to leave town."

"How old were you when you got married, Mother?" Louisa repeated.

"Age is not important. The important thing is to marry the young man God has prepared for you. And it seems that young man is Peter McClough. When he returns, all will work out for the best."

"I know you were barely seventeen, Mama, so I'm much older than you were when you and Father married. Do you want me to live with the two of you forever?"

Jack Bradford threw up his hands, and his mustache twitched above a slight smile at the corners of his mouth. "Such a thought!" he joked. "How could we bear it, Elizabeth?"

Elizabeth Bradford poked her husband playfully. "Be sensible, Jack. Louisa may take you seriously. You know how serious-minded she is. And right now she is upset about Peter's departure."

"You are joking about a very touchy subject," Louisa said as she picked up her plate and started toward the kitchen. "I have no desire to discuss this conversation further. Peter McClough is a complete cad and inconsiderate of my feelings. He didn't have the decency to stop by and say he planned to leave town. We were together yesterday, and he never mentioned a thing. In fact, we had an engagement for tomorrow evening. He planned to take me for a carriage ride by the river and then out to dinner."

"Perhaps that will still come to pass," Mr. Bradford said matter-of-factly. "Peter may return in time for your meeting tomorrow night, although it doesn't seem likely. Don't panic over something when you don't know the details. Give him the benefit of the doubt."

There was a long pause as Louisa considered her father's words. "I can't sit around and wonder when and if Peter means to return, Father! We are betrothed, and I should know about his plans for the future. He can't tamper with my feelings and expect me to ignore his neglect. Peter should have taken time to come by today and explain the circumstances surrounding his trip. He wasn't very considerate of my feelings. He could have sent a message with you when he saw you at the bank. Instead he hurries off like a house on fire!"

Louisa reflected for a few moments on the night Peter proposed. She remembered the eagerness in his boyish face as he vowed his love for her and asked her to be his bride. A quiver of excitement mounted as she mentally pictured herself once again in his arms—their lips touching in a gentle kiss. Life seemed so perfect then, as they made plans for their future together as man and wife. Her heart constricted within her breast. Why did Peter leave so quickly and without a word? Did something come up from his past that could interfere with their marriage? Was there another woman somewhere, someone he was involved with before he met her? She glanced at her parents who seemed deep in thought. Bless their hearts, they liked Peter and were encouraging and supportive. She appreciated their care, but a strange fear gripped her thoughts. What if Peter never returned?

Louisa frowned and shook her head, as if to clear her mind of such thoughts. "You're right," she said to her parents and forced a smile. "I am making too much of this. Surely I'll hear from him soon. However," she said with emphasis, "Peter McClough will have a lot of explaining to do when he gets back!"

three

Peter McClough hurriedly covered the distance from his house to Front Street and the Somerset and Kennebec Railway Station. His ticket had been purchased earlier in the day, soon after he received the wire. A frown knotted his forehead, and his lips pursed together as he let out a deep sigh. It had been a hectic morning. He took large funds out of the bank for his trip and engaged Martha, his part-time housekeeper, to watch after things at his house. He stopped by Zeke's, his occasional gardener, and requested he look after the grounds. Then he gave notice of his departure to Mr. Turner, his boss at the lumber mill.

Peter pushed back locks of dark hair which fell over his forehead and ran his hands across his brown eyes as if to clear his vision. His many hasty errands had tired him, and he groaned inwardly as he found a seat in the coach next to the window. Anxiously he pulled the crumpled wire from his coat pocket. It had been read and reread so many times it was barely legible. He fumbled with the crumpled piece of paper and smoothed it with his hands so he could read the words once again.

"Peter. Come at once. Important news about your brother."

It was signed by the distant cousin of his mother who had notified him during the war of his mother's death. She took care of the burial arrangements. Simply Annabelle Hayes. The address enclosed was a small suburb of Boston, out in the country, a place unfamiliar to him. Peter shook his head as he studied the crumpled message. He knew it by heart but needed something tangible to hold in his hands. *What is this about a brother? As far as I know, I never had a brother. Unless he was born after I left for the army. Why wasn't I told, if that were the case? Ma died in 1864. He'd be just a little chap about four years old. Whatever would I do with a kid? Who is his father? And where has he been all these years?*

Peter recrumpled the message and stuffed it back into his pocket. It puzzled him. He felt weak thinking about it, but he couldn't ignore the wire. It was important to go to the Boston area immediately and find out the details. He recalled his brief encounter with Mr. Bradford that morning and felt ashamed at his haste and mysterious attitude. But it was nothing he desired to discuss—at least at the present. He had too many questions himself and could hardly explain it to others. *What must Louisa be thinking? We had an engagement for tomorrow night for a carriage ride by the Kennebec River and dinner at our favorite restaurant. I'd planned a wonderful evening. I'll not be able to keep it, and she won't understand. Louisa, my darling, I do love you, and I'll be back.*

Peter had wired the cousin explaining he would meet with her at her address on the outskirts of Boston the following day. His hand trembled as he took out his gold pocket watch —one he inherited from his father, George McClough. It was something he cherished deeply since it belonged to the father he never knew. "It's especially dear to me since I learned what a respected man my father was," he muttered, noticing the time. He pocketed the watch hastily. "The train seems to be right on time. Good! I need to get this brother business settled once and for all."

Peter planned to arrive in Boston and take a room for the night before meeting the cousin on the morrow. A good night's sleep would help settle his nerves and prepare him for the encounter with Annabelle Hayes—and his brother. "I can never expect Louisa to marry me until this part of my life is cleared away," Peter mumbled aloud. "It wouldn't be fair to involve her. I don't know any of the details, but I may have to raise this child. He's my brother and my responsibility, but I can't ask Louisa to be strapped with a child. She may want to break our engagement when she finds out."

Peter leaned back and tried to relax as the train sped down the tracks with a rhythmic clickety-clack, clickety-clack, past the lush countryside. He took off his suit coat and laid it on the empty seat next to him—thankful to be alone. Worried, anxious, and somewhat depressed, Peter preferred not to engage in conversation with anyone. The coach looked barren—virtually empty with only a few passengers scattered here and there. Weariness overtook him as the train swayed from side to side. The methodic hum of the wheels on the track pulled at his tortured mind, and he slept fitfully for a short time. Peter smiled in his sleep during a brief dream about Louisa. They sat together in the parlor of the Bradford home. She smiled at him with her lovely smile and teased him with her wide, gray eyes. He reached for her, but a small child moved between them. He tried to reach past the child, but Louisa evaded his embrace and seemed to melt into oblivion. Peter ran after her, calling her name. His legs felt heavy, almost glued to the spot, and would not cooperate. He couldn't move! Frantically, with all his strength, he reached for her again and woke up in a deep sweat.

❧

Peter took a room in a modest, but clean, boardinghouse and went to find a decent meal. His stomach growled loudly because he hadn't eaten since breakfast. "At least I had breakfast before the wire came," he muttered. "Otherwise, I couldn't have eaten a bite." He settled himself in a small cafe on the main street and ordered a light supper. Although hungry, he ate little and turned in early—planning to eat a good breakfast the following day.

After a restless night, Peter ordered a hearty breakfast at the same small cafe where he had eaten a light supper the evening before. His mouth watered at the tasty food, and he managed to down mugs of black coffee, pancakes, and sausage. Fully satisfied, Peter set out for the livery stable on the corner. He rented a carriage and team of horses, and with directions from the stable boy, started for the country and his cousin's address.

The September air felt warm and balmy as he drove the horses along the dusty roadway out of town. Horses and cattle dotted the countryside where wide, open fields of oats and alfalfa blew in the soft breeze. Beyond the fields, wooded areas of tall trees beckoned as their lofty branches stirred and bent toward him. Peter appreciated the fresh, sweet smells around him and took long, deep breaths of air. The farms and surrounding areas reminded him of the Mason farm back in Waterville, Maine. He always loved working with his friend Frederic and Fred's father and grandfather around the farm. Many chores awaited, and the Mason family appreciated an extra hand with the plowing or harvesting. They welcomed Peter as one of their own. Peter especially enjoyed the horses and became quite adept at riding and herding the cows into the barn. Harvest time proved busy for everyone. The men brought in the crops so the womenfolk could prepare them for the long, hard winter. Jams and jellies often bubbled on the cook stove as the women ladled them into their proper containers.

Peter enjoyed none of this growing up with his mother. They lived in a small flat over a grocery store in the city of Boston. It was always hot in the summer and cold in the winter, and there was never enough food for a growing boy. But his mother always had her drinks—and reeked of it. He shuddered as he envisioned the smell—and the way she looked when drunk. Lucinda Graham, the name she went by, was a pretty woman when sober, but she neglected her son and left him alone most of the time. Evenings she dressed up in gaily colored clothing, bid him good night, and went out on the town with her men friends. Many nights he cried himself to sleep and never heard his mother come home in the wee hours of the morning.

"I couldn't wait to get away," Peter stated loudly. One of the horses jerked his head and snorted, as though Peter had given him a command. "When the war broke out between the states, I joined up with a Massachusetts regiment," Peter continued, talking audibly. "They needed every man they could get their hands on to enlist. I wasn't a very nice person in the army, but I learned some things. I obeyed the rules. I didn't desert the military like a lot of the men I knew. The army learned they could depend on me. For the first time I felt my life had a purpose. . .serving my country. The killing was terrible. . .the pain and the dying. I don't ever want to go through that again. Some of my buddies fell beside me, downed by a Reb's bullet. I can still hear their anguished moans of pain as they suffered on the battlefield, bled, and died." Peter brushed a hand across his forehead as if to blot out the memory. "There was nothing I could do. . .nothing anyone could do to save them. Both the North and the South suffered through those bloody battles. But God, I know You protected me through the war. Rotten as I was, and not worth a cent, You kept me alive. I'll be forever grateful, Lord. There must be some purpose for my life. Show me what it is. My highest desire is to have my life count for You."

Peter studied his directions from the stable boy, ones he had hastily scribbled on the back of his wire. "Ho, there boys," he shouted to the horses while pulling on their reins. "We need to make a turn here and go yonder down thataway."

Annabelle Hayes's address led him to a small, white cottage with green shutters and trim. It looked very neat and inviting as Peter stepped down from the carriage and secured the horses to the hitching post. It lay at the side of the house with ample grazing area and a water trough for his team. At his knock a middle-aged woman appeared—her dark hair pulled back at the nape of her neck in a bun. She was pleasantly plump, with a round, jolly face and big smile. Her eyes rolled up at the corners with delight when she spied Peter.

"Peter!" she cried, throwing her arms around the tall young man. "I'd know you anywhere! It's so good to see you."

"But. . . ," Peter sputtered at this sudden show of affection, "I don't know you, do I? Have we ever met before?"

"I'm Annabelle Hayes, your mother's second cousin. I've seen glimpses of you through the years, Peter. Your mother would never let me visit, but I caught sight of you at times whenever I could without your knowing I was kinfolk. Once in a while, I happened to see you in town—from a distance. Other times I viewed you playing with friends behind the store where you lived. You do bear a resemblance to Lucy. I'm her only kinfolk except for you. . .and Thomas."

"I don't understand why she never allowed you to visit us," Peter said. "I would have welcomed a visit to you and your quaint little cottage in the country. It's so different from my mother's stuffy flat over the grocery store. And who is Thomas? Is that my so-called brother?"

"Come inside, Peter, and we'll talk," Annabelle said leading him inside the neat dwelling. "I have some lunch prepared and a cool drink. You must be hungry."

"Thank you, Mrs. Hayes."

Annabelle Hayes laughed a hearty, rippling laugh that went on and on. "It's so good of you to come. I feared you wouldn't. And please call me Annabelle. We're kinfolk, you know."

Peter glanced around the well-kept cottage at the plain, but sturdy furniture. His eyes lingered on a large oval portrait of a young man and woman. It hung prominently above the small stone fireplace. The face of the young woman looked vaguely familiar. "Is this you in the portrait, Mrs. Hayes. . .er Annabelle? I believe I see a likeness there."

Annabelle Hayes' laugh tinkled merrily once again. "Yes, Peter, that's me and my husband, Thomas Hayes, when we were married some thirty-five years ago. I'm surprised you recognized me, though. I've put on so much weight since then."

"You haven't changed much, Annabelle," Peter said kindly. "I see the same sweet smile and merry glow about the eyes. I'm sure your wedding was a happy occasion."

"Indeed, it was," Annabelle agreed. "There's a bowl and pitcher in the back room so you can freshen up, Peter. Meanwhile, I'll get our meal on the table."

After Peter refreshed himself, he returned to the kitchen and sat down at the small pine table. Annabelle busied herself putting out plates of ham, cheese, preserves, and huge chunks of homemade bread and butter. Peter noticed there were only two places set at the table.

"Where is your husband, Thomas?" he asked. "I would surely like to meet him."

Annabelle ladled out two bowls of chicken soup and two mugs of cool apple cider. "I have much to tell you, Peter," she said taking his hand. "Would you mind if we return thanks for our food first?"

Peter smiled broadly and squeezed Annabelle's hand. "Not at all. I'm happy to hear you want to thank God for our food."

Annabelle murmured a soft prayer of thanks for Peter's safe arrival, for God's goodness and daily benefits, and for the food. When she glanced up, her eyes were moist.

"Peter, you must be a changed young man. From things your mother told me about you before her death, I understood you hated God with a vengeance—as she did."

"I did, Annabelle," Peter said buttering a large chunk of homemade bread. "Mother brought me up to be bitter against God. She said He had ruined her life and that was the reason we had nothing, not enough food or clothing at times. She always looked out for herself, though. She had enough money for drinks. . .and clothes to entice her men friends."

"What happened, Peter? Did you accept the Lord on the battlefield? I've heard many young men turned to God during wartime, especially in the southern ranks. General Robert E.

Lee and other leaders in the North and South were fine Christians. Many of the Southern camps held special evangelistic meetings. That was such a tragic war between the northern and southern states. Brother against brother, sometimes." Annabelle's face gathered into a frown, and she shuddered slightly.

"No, I didn't meet God on the battlefield, Annabelle. I should have. God certainly looked out for me and kept me safe. I was a wretched individual in the army, crude and miserable to most of the people around me. . .especially if they believed in God. It happened when I went to Waterville, Maine, to claim my inheritance left to me by my father, George McClough."

Peter continued, between mouthfuls, to explain the influence the Mason family had in leading him to the Lord. He told Annabelle he mistrusted their kindness at first and thought they wanted part of the inheritance. "Originally it went to the Mason family because George's second wife, Maude, was Mr. Mason's sister. It was when Maude died, several years after my father died, that his lawyer located me as sole heir to George's estate."

"Did that upset the Mason family?" Annabelle asked. "It seems an unexpected loss might anger some folk."

"They were wonderful about it. At the time, it seemed unreal to me. How could anyone be nice to someone who took away their inheritance? But their attitude was so kind. They are Christians and treated me like family. Frederic, the son, is my dearest friend. He and his young wife, Sarah, cared about me and my future even though I had treated Fred rotten in the army. I grew to love the entire Mason family. I owe them a great debt of gratitude. Because of their example, their lives of faith, I eventually found peace with God by trusting Jesus as my Savior."

"Praise God," Annabelle whispered. "My prayers for you have been answered after all these years."

"Annabelle," Peter said with emotion, "You prayed for me all these years? I never knew I had anyone who cared about me, let alone who prayed for me, except for the Masons during these later years. Did you pray for my mother, also?"

"Yes, I did. Your mother was a lovely person at one time. We were close growing up, but we had different ideals, different views on life. Lucinda was the pretty one. I was plain beside her. She desired money, clothes, entertainment—anything this world had to offer. She changed from a sweet, young girl to an aggressive, greedy woman of the world. Her values and her morals were warped. But all I could do was pray. She wouldn't listen."

"If she had only stayed with my father," Peter said thoughtfully, "our lives would have been so different. I understand he was a fine Christian man and well-respected as a doctor in Waterville."

"He certainly was," Annabelle agreed. "I knew your father well when he had his medical practice here in Boston. I was never able to have children, and I doctored with Dr. McClough for several years."

"Did you finally have a child, Annabelle?"

"I was never able to conceive my own child," Annabelle said sadly. "But Dr. McClough was not to be faulted. There seemed to be no explanation for my lack of childbearing. It was in God's hands, and someday I'll understand. He knows what is best."

"I'm sorry, Annabelle. I'm sure you would have been a wonderful mother."

"Your mother met George when she accompanied me on my many visits to his office in town. They talked together often, and Dr. McClough started courting her soon after. The couple didn't know each other well when he asked her to marry him. Your father was such a fine man. I assumed Lucy would change. My heart sank when Lucy told me she'd married him because he had more money than any other man she knew. And he was well-respected in Boston. It was a big step up for her, she said. Now she would be somebody!"

Peter rested his elbows on the table and bent his head into his hands. When he looked up, his eyes were moist. "What happened, Annabelle? Why didn't my mother stay with my father?"

"George McClough, a fine Christian, did not tolerate drinking, not even socially. He saw what it did to people. . . especially some of his patients who drank all their lives and ended up with liver problems. Lucinda drank. She never let go of it for him or anyone else. God never entered the picture. 'Why would God want to keep me from having fun?' she'd ask. Lucy hid drink around the house, drinking when George was away at his office or on calls. I never knew where she got it, but she had connections, certain friends who kept her supplied."

"Didn't things change when I came along?" Peter asked. "Was my mother happy about my birth?"

"I'm sorry, Peter, but that's when the marriage fell apart. Your mother didn't want to be tied down with a child. She resented you, but she wouldn't let George McClough have you. She seemed to go out of her mind with hatred toward him. She said he'd ruined her life. Lucy expected to have a soft life as Dr. McClough's wife. 'I'll be queen of the social world when I marry George McClough,' she told me once. 'We'll be wining and dining all the important people of Boston, Annabelle, and you'll be so envious of me.' I tried to reason with her, but to no avail.

"Your father was delighted with your birth and expected Lucy to stay home, give up her drinking, and tend to their son. They were from two different worlds, Peter. It's very sad. George McClough could never visit or see his only son. Lucy didn't want you, but she refused to allow your father the privilege of raising you. She moved the two of you out of the large brick house he'd provided and moved into the cheap flat above the grocery store."

"I wonder about the divorce lawyer," Peter said thought-fully. "Didn't he know the kind of woman my mother was? It's obvious my father should have raised me. How different my life could have been."

"George McClough said nothing against Lucy to taint her character. I'm sure the lawyer, a new man in town, knew nothing of her past. The divorce was a mutual agreement between them. Your father agreed to give Lucy a large sum of money and send a very substantial monthly support payment until you reached age eighteen. Dr. McClough left Boston soon afterward and took up his medical profession in Waterville, Maine. Boston lost a good doctor, and Waterville gained a fine one. Lucy could have lived well with the money George gave her and his monthly support payments. Instead she fell into a life of drinking and degradation. She held onto you so she could count on George's support money. It was a good amount of money on the first of each month, but she frittered it away. Lucy wasn't concerned with your best interests, Peter. I'm sorry to be the one to tell you. It's sad, but true."

Peter pounded his left hand with his right fist. "Why did I have such a rotten mother?" He pounded his fist once again. "Why couldn't I have had a mother like you, Annabelle? You wanted a child desperately and couldn't have one. My mother didn't want me but kept me as a hold on my father's pocketbook. Life seems so unfair sometimes."

"Don't be bitter, Peter," Annabelle soothed, patting his arm. "We'll never understand the why of everything in this life. All life's trials can be turned into good by resting them in God's hands. He knows about our heartaches, and He cares."

Peter's face relaxed. "I know, Annabelle. I'm still learning about God and His ways. I've been studying religion at Colby College in Waterville. I should probably go to a Bible school, but I haven't wanted to leave the area. I work at the mill in Waterville and go to Colby part-time. I'm unsure about my future. I'd like to be involved in the Lord's work, somehow. I'm just waiting on Him for direction in my life."

"That's commendable, Peter. It makes me happy to hear you talk about God and a desire to serve Him in some way. He will use you mightily if you'll follow His leading."

"But Annabelle, you never answered my question about your husband, Thomas. Where is he? And I need to know about my brother. Do I really have a brother? I'm anxious to meet him. He must have been born while I was at war. I'd guess he's about four years old. Where is the little fella?"

Annabelle's eyes widened, and her mouth dropped open, then her round face broke into a merry laugh that went on and on, crinkling her eyes up in the corners. "Oh, Peter," she said as her face grew more serious. "Your brother is not here at this time. Come, let's get more comfortable on the sofa. There is so much I've yet to tell you."

four

Annabelle settled down on the mohair sofa and folded and refolded her hands. "It's quite a story, Peter. I hardly know where to begin."

"I want to hear everything," Peter said seriously, sitting beside her. "This part of my life is a mystery to me. It's important to know all the facts because they are part of my heritage. Don't hold anything back."

Annabelle glanced upward as though uttering a silent prayer, took a deep breath, and began to speak softly. "Lucinda, your mother, had a baby boy before she met your father. Your half brother is not a mere child, Peter. He is a grown man. Your mother was not married at the time, and the baby's father did not stay around to see his child."

Peter gasped slightly as he took in everything Annabelle said. "What happened to him? Didn't my father know about this child when he married my mother?"

"No, he never knew Lucy had a son. He was only a babe in arms when she accompanied me on my visits to Dr. McClough. She always left him with one of her so-called lady friends."

"But my father had to know later, Annabelle. She couldn't hide him from my father after they were married."

"She could and she did, Peter. When Dr. McClough showed interest in Lucy, she decided it was her big chance. Through marriage to an important doctor in the community, the upper class would welcome her into Boston's social arena. This meant a great deal to Lucinda. She begged me to take the child and raise him as my own. Dr. McClough was never to know my foster son was hers. It would ruin her chances for a better life, she said. The boy was too young to

35

know what was happening. She said if I took him, it would be better for all concerned."

"How could she do that, Annabelle? How can a woman give up her child and not care deeply?"

"I think she honestly hoped to start over and make a new life for herself with your father, but she fell back into her old ways and ruined your father's life as well. Lucy made Thomas and me promise, if we took the child, to never come around them or tell anyone whose child it was. Eager to have a child, I didn't hesitate at her offer. We agreed to take the little tyke and raise him as our own. We loved him dearly, Peter. A delightful child, he grew in our hearts. We named him Thomas after my husband. He is only a year and a half older than you."

Peter's brow knitted into a scowl. He spat out angry words. "The more I hear about my mother, the more I hate her. She was the worst kind of a mother. I knew she never cared about me, but to give up her first son without a backward glance is too much."

"Don't harbor hate, Peter. It eats away at your insides and makes you a bitter person. You don't want to go through life with a bitter spirit."

Peter bent forward and placed his head in his hands as he struggled to control his emotions. "Life is full of surprises, Annabelle. Just when I thought my life was all straightened out and going well, this happens. Now the old feelings toward my mother are alive again and real. They cut into me like a knife. I dealt with them long ago and put them behind me. But today they taunt me again. Is there more to this story?"

"There is, Peter, but let's take a walk first. It will clear your mind to get out in the fresh air, and I need some exercise. The doctor tells me to walk a little every day."

Peter jumped up and stretched. "I'm sure a walk will be good for both of us. Are you quite well, Annabelle? It sounds as though you are under a doctor's care."

"I'm fine," she said pulling off her apron and hanging it over a chair. "It's this roly-poly body of mine." Annabelle patted her midsection, smoothed her full calico skirts and placed a bonnet on her head. "The doctor tells me I mustn't gain any more weight, or I'll waddle like a duck. He's a young whippersnapper, but a fine doctor. And he's right, of course. I need to lose some weight and keep active."

They went out the kitchen door, and Annabelle closed it tightly behind her. Peter went to the pump and drew fresh water for the team of horses. The horses snorted and stamped their feet as he approached and poured water into the trough. "Thirsty, aren't you, fellas?" Peter asked, and he watched them as they took long drinks and jerked their heads up and down. "Mind if I give them a few of your apples, Annabelle?" Peter asked, gesturing toward the apple tree nearby. "They must be hungry by now." When Annabelle nodded her okay, Peter picked some juicy, red apples from a nearby tree. "Here you go, boys," he said, cupping his hands, which were full of apples. The horses shook their heads up and down and neighed when they saw the fruit. Peter patted their heads for a few moments as they ate heartily, chewing and drooling apple juice. Deep in thought, Peter mulled over all the latest details about his mother.

Finally Annabelle approached him and took his arm. "Come with me, Peter," she said as she guided him away from the horses. "It's time for our walk."

The couple followed the gravel road several hundred feet and then turned onto a country path. It was quiet and still, but Peter noticed a farmhouse in the distance and the cattle and horses grazing in the pasture. Although the path rolled gently over hill and vale, Annabelle walked it with no difficulty. Peter followed the short, stocky figure ahead of him, amazed at her quick and determined pace. A small creek ran alongside the trail gurgling merrily as it bubbled over rocks and tree roots. Overhead a flock of geese honked noisily as they gracefully headed south.

"This is a shortcut," Annabelle stated.

"Where are we going?" Peter asked. "Anywhere in particular, or just a leisurely stroll on a warm, September afternoon?"

"A grove of trees lies up ahead and then you'll see the church. It's nestled into the countryside yonder just beyond a bend in the trail. Our little country church, the one Thomas and I attended with little Thomas, is very special. I remember many happy years of fellowship with God's people in this place."

Peter looked ahead and spotted a sharp bend in the path. The trail was well-worn, and he decided Annabelle must walk it often. It was a shortcut, she'd said. It would be nice to see the church his brother attended with Annabelle and her husband. *My brother must be a Christian. I'm sure Annabelle and her husband saw to that. Wonderful! We'll have something in common besides having the same mother. I wonder if Thomas knows Annabelle isn't his real mother.*

"Is your husband, Thomas, the pastor of the church, Annabelle? I'm looking forward to meeting him."

Annabelle stopped abruptly. They had rounded a bend in the trail. Peter saw the little white church up ahead, complete with steeple and bell. The church stood near a grove of trees and next to the church, shaded by some of the trees, lay a small cemetery. It was fenced on all sides with a gate at the front. The cemetery appeared very neat and well-kept.

"My husband Thomas is here," Annabelle said pointing toward the little cemetery. She noted the questions in Peter's eyes and hastened to explain. "He died several years ago and was buried in the little graveyard next to our church."

Peter's face registered pain and he reached out to her. "I'm so sorry, Annabelle. I. . .I don't know what to say."

Annabelle smiled up at him. "It's all right, Peter," she said patting his arm. "Of course I miss my husband dearly. We had a beautiful life together. But Thomas suffered so much with his illness, it was heartbreaking. His death ended all that. And he isn't here, actually, you know. He's with Jesus, which is far better."

"Yes, Annabelle," Peter agreed, as he swallowed the lump in his throat. "Far better."

Annabelle led Peter through the little gate and down one of the long rows. She stopped in front of a plot with a small stone marker. Flowers still bloomed on the grave.

"I come here every day," she said softly, "unless I am ill or snowed in. I need the walk, and I feel closer to Thomas. . . even though I know his spirit is with God."

"It's a peaceful setting for a cemetery," Peter said as he took in the beauty of the surrounding area. His eyes lingered on the hills and valleys that were dotted with contented cows and grazing horses. "It seems so restful here."

The couple stood quietly for several moments before Annabelle tugged at his arm. "Your mother is buried here, Peter. Would you like to see her grave?"

Peter grimaced. He felt the old bitterness fill his spirit and weigh him down. Tempted to refuse, he hesitated until Annabelle broke into his thoughts.

"You'll feel better if you see where we laid her. I was able to bury Lucy here because she is a relative of mine. I asked her many times, but she never did attend our little church."

Quickly Peter pushed the ill feelings out of his mind and followed Annabelle down another path. She stood before another small plot, well-kept and complete with flowers and headstone.

"I keep Lucy's grave just as I do Thomas's. Lucy didn't treat me well in later years, but we were close growing up. I have fond memories of our early years together. I tried, but I could never reach her with the gospel." Annabelle sighed heavily. "This is my one regret concerning our relationship."

Peter stood spellbound and gazed at the tombstone. LUCINDA GRAHAM 1820–1864. "My mother was only forty-four years old when she died," he said softly. Suddenly his shoulders convulsed as tears flowed down his cheeks. With head in hands, he sobbed uncontrollably for a few minutes.

Annabelle moved toward him and placed an arm around his waist.

"It's good for you to cry, Peter. Let the tears come and get it out of your system. God washes away the dross and bitterness in our hearts. We need His cleansing power every day. Without it, we'd lose our sweet fellowship with Him."

Peter pulled out his bandana and wiped away tears from his reddened eyes. A few deep shudders shook his body. "I needed this, Annabelle, and I feel better now. When I saw my mother's grave, I felt anger rear its ugly head inside me again. But I refuse to harbor bitterness. I will not let anger get the best of me or control my life. I make this promise to you, and to God, here and now."

Annabelle showed her delight at Peter's promise with a bright smile as they walked arm in arm toward the little church. They went inside the small building and sat quietly on one of the benches for a few moments. A few chairs sat on the platform at the front. The wooden stand, built to hold the pastor's Bible, was centered on the platform. Just below the platform, a large Bible rested on a table covered with a white linen cloth.

"I come here often and just sit for a spell. I feel close to God and to Thomas. It isn't a fancy church, Peter, but it's God's house, and we worship here."

Peter closed his eyes for a few moments. "I can picture you and Thomas, with my brother Thomas, worshipping here. I wish I'd attended with you, Annabelle. If only my life had been different."

"We can't live in the past or on the 'if only's,' Peter. The past is over and done. We must see what God has for us in the present and then look to the future."

"You're right," Peter said eagerly as he stood up. "I need to meet my brother, Thomas, and see what the future holds for us. Is he anxious to meet me, Annabelle? Where do we go from here?"

Annabelle remained unusually quiet on their walk back to her cottage. She led Peter at a fast pace along the well-traveled path. Back at the house she dropped breathless onto the overstuffed, mohair sofa and motioned Peter to do the same.

"Is something wrong with my brother?" Peter asked as he settled beside her. "Is that why you asked me to come?"

"Yes and no," Annabelle said, searching his face. "Thomas visited me a month ago and seemed fine. But he took off without saying where he planned to go, and I haven't heard from him since."

"But Annabelle, if he isn't here, why did you send for me?"

"Selfishness, I suppose," she answered—her face downcast. "I thought perhaps you could locate him for me. And I also wanted to see you, Peter. I didn't think you'd come to see a distant cousin of your mother unless you had a good reason. Would you?"

Peter's brow knitted as he glanced at his newfound cousin. "Probably not, Annabelle. I'm involved in college classes and work some days at the sawmill. I'm also courting a lovely young lady, and we are engaged to be married."

Annabelle's face drooped, and her eyes blurred with tears. "I'm sorry," she whispered, patting his hand. "But I did so want to meet you."

"Don't be sorry, Annabelle. I'm glad I came. I'd never have met you otherwise. You've helped me get over the bitter feelings I felt toward my mother."

"Thank you, Peter," she murmured softly. "Now, I'll share some things about your brother. Thomas lived with my husband and me until he was ten. At that time my husband became ill with a serious lung disease and needed my full-time care. Lucinda decided to take Thomas away from us. She used my husband's illness as an excuse, but I believe it was the Christian training he received while in our care. Young Thomas had received Jesus into his life and knew many Bible verses. Lucy visited one day to see the extent of my husband's condition while you were at school. She didn't want you to know anything about Thomas. Lucy stayed for tea and remained long enough for the lad to return from the little schoolhouse up near the church. He only knew Lucy as a visiting friend at that time, not as his birth mother. Thomas was an outspoken child, and he talked to her about Jesus. This infuriated Lucy. A week later she arrived with a friend, and they took your brother away. He cried and clung to us, but Lucy forced him to go. My husband and I cried but could do nothing. We didn't have any right actually. We had never signed any papers. He wasn't legally ours. Thomas was her child. She waved his birth record in our faces and left." Tears flowed freely down Annabelle's cheeks as she recalled the incident.

Clumsily Peter reached for her. A few shudders convulsed her body. Suddenly she straightened up, wiped her eyes, and blew her nose. "I'm all right now," she whispered.

"Did you ever find out what happened to him?" Peter asked. "My mother never brought him home. As far as I knew, I was her only son."

"Lucy visited me again several months later." Little sobs caught in Annabelle's throat as she fought for control. "Lucy's friend took Thomas and moved back to the South where her parents lived. Your mother insisted he was well taken care of. The woman's family lived on a large plantation, which boasted many slaves. Thomas would be brought up as a Southern gentleman and never need for a thing. A poor boy turned rich, your mother said."

Peter shook his head. "Didn't it make you angry, Annabelle? You must have hated my mother at that time."

"No, my husband and I didn't hate her. We were sad, though. Thomas, the boy, and Thomas, the father, were very close. They had a special relationship which only happens between a father and a son. We both loved him dearly and felt a tremendous loss. But we also felt sad for Lucinda. She continued to seek her own way in the things of this world.

Instead of becoming bitter, my husband and I prayed for her. It's the only way, Peter. Otherwise our lives become a poor testimony to His grace."

"Of course, Annabelle, you're right. I can't imagine you being bitter toward anyone."

Annabelle stood up and dabbed away at her teary, red eyes. "I'll fix us some tea and continue my story. Do you have to get the team back to the stable tonight?"

"Yes. I have my room reserved for one more night."

"Why don't you move your things out here tomorrow, Peter? You can have your brother's old room. It's just the way he left it when he was ten years old."

Peter hesitated and rubbed his chin thoughtfully. "It won't hurt to stay a few days, Annabelle. I'd appreciate being your guest."

Annabelle beamed, and her merry little laugh echoed forth. "You aren't a guest, Peter. You're kin, remember?"

While Annabelle continued her tale, they sipped the brewed tea and ate homemade sugar cookies. She told him her husband died without seeing young Thomas again. It had been such a difficult time for him, being ill, and missing the lad so much. Annabelle felt it hastened his demise.

"Lucy refused to give me young Thomas's address in the South. When my husband died, I begged her to release the information, and she finally agreed. He was fifteen by this time. I sent a letter explaining my husband's death and asked Thomas to write me."

"Did he write you?" Peter asked eagerly.

"He didn't write at first. But I wrote him again and reminded him of some things from his childhood. I hoped this would spark his interest, and it did. I received a brief note. He hardly knew what to say. After all, it had been five years. But he told me about the plantation and all the slaves who worked for them. He didn't go to a school but had a teacher at home instead. He had a special slave his own age, Ben, assigned to him who did all the menial tasks. Although Ben waited on him, Thomas said Ben was his friend. He spoke highly of him. They fished together in the creek, rode horses around the plantation, climbed trees, and spent much of their time together."

"That sounds like another world, Annabelle. Did Thomas ever come to see you during that time?"

"He was twenty before he looked me up. I was delighted. It was early in 1861 before the War Between the States. Thomas couldn't understand all the fuss about slavery. He was very confused. He thought war was inevitable, though, because there was so much dissension among the plantation owners. Their anger against the union had reached a new high. The North felt slavery had to be dealt with, and the South rebelled.

"It was a sweet reunion for young Thomas and me after ten years, Peter. He'd grown so tall and handsome. Thomas feared the slavery problem would separate the country because the South felt so strongly in favor of it. He said the South was ready to pull away and build their own government. I tried to impress him with the evil of slavery according to the Bible. I reminded him that all God's people are equal and precious in His sight."

"Did he agree with you? What was his reaction?"

"He'd been away from Bible training and church a long time. But Thomas agreed keeping slaves was wrong. He felt badly for them, especially when they were disciplined or separated from their family. His friend Ben's parents had been sold to another plantation owner, and Ben grieved for them. Whenever Thomas mentioned these things to the plantation owner, his foster father, the man laughed at him. The master argued that his father had slaves before him and his father before that. 'Who'll do all the work?' the master asked Thomas. 'No, lad, we've always had slaves and always will. We'll fight the North and win!' Thomas didn't agree with him, but there was nothing he could do. The master of the plantation had been Thomas's foster father for ten years. He had a certain amount of love and respect for the man. The Civil War started a few months later."

"Did my brother go to war, Annabelle? Surely he wanted to save the union and fight for the North. He'd want his friend free to reunite with his family and break the bonds of servitude."

"I received a letter from him after the war started. Thomas felt a sense of duty toward his homeland, the South, even though he despised slavery. He enlisted with the Confederates and fought bravely with the men from Tennessee. The South believed in their cause just as the North did. Of course I never saw Thomas during the war. He wrote me a few other times and revealed the hardships. There were too many to describe. When the men marched, some had no shoes. The conditions were deplorable. They had a shortage of food, and men nearly starved to death. A great number died from disease and dysentery. It was a terrible war."

Peter frowned. "My brother was a Reb! I fought this war against my own brother! I probably faced him across the battlefield! We might have killed each other, Annabelle!"

"I prayed for you both. You didn't know it, of course, but I prayed. And Thomas knew because I wrote him often and told him so. I reminded him of his Christian background and his decision as a child to follow the Lord. Although he had to kill or be killed, I urged him to stay close to God."

"If you saw him a month ago, God brought him through it. . . just as He did me. I'm thankful I didn't know I had a brother fighting for the South. I couldn't have faced each confrontation on the battlefield knowing my brother might be fighting in the field across from me. It would have been more than I could have borne."

"God knows how much we can bear, Peter. Perhaps that's one reason He kept you and Thomas apart all those years."

"Did Thomas go back to his plantation after the war? What happened to the slaves? They were given their freedom, weren't they?"

"Thomas went back to Tennessee in 1865 after the war ended. John Berringer, the master of the plantation, had passed away. Thomas's foster father went quite out of his mind when the war didn't go well for the South. His wife had passed away earlier. From then on, he went downhill and finally died. Your mother's young friend, the one who took Thomas away from us, had married and left the plantation several years before her parents' death. Thomas said the house, neglected and run down, appeared almost haunted. All the slaves, free at last, had scattered except for his friend, Ben. Ben married after Thomas left for the war, and he and his family settled in one of the small slaver's cabins. Faithful to his friend, Ben wouldn't leave without seeing Thomas again. Their friendship went too deep. He determined to help Thomas repair the big house and make it livable once more. The two friends worked side by side on the house and re-planted some of the fields. Then the two men built a much larger cabin for Ben and his family."

"It sounds like my brother is a nice fellow, Annabelle. He showed concern and appreciation for his friend. I'm glad to hear good things about Thomas."

Annabelle glanced away and Peter noticed a sadness cloud her eyes. "Thomas is in deep trouble, Peter. That's another reason I asked you to come. I hoped you could help him."

"What is it? Does he need money to get his plantation going again? My father left me well-off. Of course I'll help him!"

Annabelle blurted out the next words. "Thomas killed a man in Tennessee and fled the area. He stopped here last month and told me about the incident. I asked him to stay here with me until we could decide what to do. After a few days, he left secretly during the night, and I haven't heard from him since. He worried about getting me involved in his problem, Peter. That's why he left. He wanted to spare me any trouble."

Peter let out a low whistle. "Thomas killed a man! But Annabelle, there must have been a reason!"

five

"Why I declare!" Louisa announced as she fumbled with the mail. "It's a letter from Emily out in Pennsylvania. Isn't that grand?" She waved a pink envelope for her mother to see, then hastened to tear it open. "I've been waiting for this!"

"Your friend has been busy, dear, getting settled," Mrs. Bradford said. "They've only been married a short time. What does she have to say?"

The pair settled themselves on the plush damask sofa in the parlor, and Louisa read her friend's letter aloud.

"Dear Louisa,

We are still getting settled, but I wanted to write you as soon as possible. Robert and I are living in a sweet little cottage which belongs to a family in the church. It is small but adequate for our needs. The cottage has two bedrooms and is furnished with sturdy and comfortable furniture. Windows are decked with gay, calico curtains, which makes the place seem bright and cheery. It's almost hard to believe I am finally married. Remember what a difficult person I was? I didn't want to come to Pennsylvania at all, and it almost prevented our marriage. I'm thankful Robert's patience held out long enough for me to come to my senses. Wampum is a lovely rural area and reminds me much of where I lived on my family's farm outside of Waterville. The countryside is lush and fertile. Wide, green pastures are dotted with cattle and horses, and you know how much I love horses. I should be able to ride to my heart's content. Beaver Creek is bigger than our creek at home, and fish are abundant in the stream. We are very happy, Louisa, and I heartily recommend married life. I like being a pastor's wife. Robert is such a dear, a very caring and helpful husband.

"The women at the church are so kind. They held a reception for us and showered us with wedding gifts. Many gifts are homemade, charming, and special. Their expression of love made me feel accepted as one of them. I appreciate their friendship. As a pastor's wife, everything is new to me. Pray that I will be a good pastor's wife. I want to be a helpmate to my husband as he cares for the flock here in Wampum.

"There is a troublemaker in the church, Jim Bishop. He is a thorn in Robert's flesh. Mr. Bishop tries to be in control. He is a very manipulative person. Everything must be done his way. Mrs. Bishop seems sweet. She is very quiet and shy. I'm afraid her husband domineers her also. Their two children fear their father. I can see it in their eyes. Please pray about this situation. Robert needs wisdom to deal with this problem.

"How is everything in Waterville? I miss you, my family, and friends. But this is where God wants me—with Robert and the ministry in Wampum. Can you believe I said that, when I was so opposed to it at one time? But I am content, dear Louisa, and at peace. Have you and Peter set the date for your wedding yet? Robert and I rejoiced when we heard the good news about your engagement. I remember Peter seemed very dreamy and nostalgic when Robert and I married. We thought that young man had some serious thoughts going on in his mind. The two of you make a charming couple. I will love having you as mistress of Peter's house, the home which previously belonged to my Aunt Maude and Uncle George. When I lived with Maudie before her death, I grew to appreciate her fine taste in furniture, china, and

*paintings. It gives me joy to know you, my dear friend,
will be taking care of them. Peter does well enough for a
man, but my aunt's home needs a woman's touch. Don't
you agree? Let me hear from you soon.*

*"With love, your close friend,
Emily"*

Louisa quietly refolded the letter and tucked it back into
the envelope. "Emily sounds blissfully happy in her new
home, Mother. I knew she'd be content once she arrived. She
really baiked at the move. . .away from family and friends in
Waterville. But as long as she and Robert are together, nothing else matters, does it?"

"Emily's learned to be satisfied in a new place with her
new husband," Elizabeth Bradford agreed. "She's started a
new life in Pennsylvania and has adjusted well. It was a good
letter. She sounded cheerful and content. I'm glad, aren't
you?"

Louisa looked down at her lap for several moments. When
she lifted her head, tears stood in the corners of her eyes.
Quickly she brushed them away. "I am happy for Emily. She
and Robert are together. . .married. . .and everything worked
out well for her. Why can't things go smoothly for me? Here
I am, with my best friend married and living far away. To
make matters worse, Peter deserted me without a word.
Emily asked if there is to be a wedding soon. What do I tell
her? No, Emily, Peter is gone, and no one knows why or
when he plans to return."

"He'll be back, Louisa," Mrs. Bradford said rising from the
sofa. "His home is here. He enrolled at Colby College again
this fall, and there is his job at the mill. He won't neglect his
commitments."

"He neglected his appointment with me." Louisa flashed
angrily. "Evidently Peter thinks I'm not important. He didn't
send a note or stop by to explain. It seems there are more

interesting things to occupy his mind."

"What's all the fuss, Louisa?" Jack Bradford asked as he entered the room. "You sound as though you are in a foul mood today."

"Hello, dear," Mrs. Bradford said, as she rose and kissed her husband briefly on the cheek. "How was your day at the bank?"

"Fine as usual, Elizabeth. But I overheard a little of your conversation with Louisa. Are things not going well at home?"

"Everything's fine, Jack. Louisa is still a little upset with Peter McClough. Nothing serious, though."

"It is serious, Father," Louisa pouted. "I don't like being neglected by Peter. Today I received a nice letter from my friend, Emily, in Pennsylvania. She asked me if Peter and I had set a wedding date, and I don't even know where he is."

Jack Bradford loosened his necktie and took off his suit coat. "Well, I have a little news for you. Not much, mind you."

Louisa's face brightened. "What is it, Father? Do you know where he is?"

"He's in Boston visiting a distant cousin. His housekeeper came into the bank this afternoon. I noticed Martha from my office, thought she might have some news, and went out to greet her."

"What did she say? Why did he go? When is he coming back?" Louisa cried, somewhat breathlessly.

"Martha received a wire from him this morning. She doesn't know any details. Peter said he will not return for a while and asked her to mind the house. It sounded as though he will be gone indefinitely."

"That is so inconsiderate!" Louisa exclaimed. "He hasn't notified me at all! I must not be very important!"

Mr. Bradford cupped his daughter's face in his hands and looked into her wide, gray eyes. "You are very important to your mother and me. As our only child, you've been our whole life. Don't let this young man upset you, Louisa."

Louisa laid her blond head against her father's shoulder, and he gathered her close. A few sobs escaped her lips as she spoke. "You and Mother have always been here for me to lean on. I appreciate your love and care. Forgive me for being such a silly goose."

"I've a great idea," Jack Bradford said. "Let's pack up and visit my brother's family in Augusta next week. They've invited us several times. I'll send them a wire tomorrow. A change will do us all good."

"But Jack," Elizabeth protested, "are you able to leave the bank at this time? Aren't you being a little hasty about all this?"

"Not at all," Jack Bradford said adjusting his spectacles. "Remember the new assistant I told you about? The young man started work two weeks ago and has proved a fine worker. He has taken to the business extremely well, and I wouldn't hesitate to leave him in charge for a time. How does a trip away from here sound to you, Louisa?"

"It sounds wonderful, Father, thank you. I'm sure it will chase away my gloominess to see cousin Clara. And it's always fun to visit Uncle Phil and Aunt Lydia. I wish they didn't live so far away."

"Then it's all settled," Jack Bradford said. He picked up his coat and tie from the chair and paused. "I'll pick up our train tickets tomorrow, and we can leave on Monday. We can stay all week if you like."

Louisa whirled about the room a few times. "I haven't seen Clara in ages, Mother. It should be great fun to be together. We'll have so much to talk about. When we visit one another, we talk nonstop!"

Elizabeth Bradford smiled as she watched the change in her daughter. Louisa's once pouty and downcast face was alive again. Her gray eyes twinkled with anticipation, and her face stretched into a wide smile. She twirled around the room a few more times until she fell on the plush sofa, completely out of breath.

"I'm glad to see you cheerful once again, Louisa," her mother said. "But Jack, are you sure about this new assistant of yours? He's only worked for you a short time, and you know nothing of his background. Did he have any references for you?"

"Not really," Jack Bradford admitted as he headed for the stairway. "But he served in the Civil War, and that's enough of a reference for me. He's only done odd jobs since then until now. He'd like very much to be settled here, and he seems likable enough."

"Oh, please, Mother," Louisa begged. "Don't discourage Father. This trip will be so good for me. I need to get out of Waterville for a spell. And if Peter does contact me, I won't be sitting around moping over him."

Elizabeth looked from her husband to her daughter and knew she was outnumbered. "Well, dear, if that's what you want. You and Clara have always been close even though we don't see the Phillip Bradford family very often. I suppose it's because you are the only cousins in the family and practically the same age. Isn't Clara only six months older than you are?"

"Yes, and she's not married yet either. It's sad her friend, Douglas Meakin, was killed in the battle at Gettysburg during the war. They weren't really engaged, but they had an understanding. Douglas felt they should wait to declare their engagement. Clara knew they were in love and would marry after the war was over. She told me in a recent letter she is not interested in meeting other men. She is still in love with her memories."

"But she needs to get over Douglas," Elizabeth Bradford said seriously. "She mustn't live in the past. Clara is a sweet, lovely young woman. I thought she would surely be over him by now. It's been years. She must realize Douglas is gone and won't be coming back. It's a matter of accepting the fact. I believe it will be good for us to go to Augusta, after all. If anyone can help Clara, it is probably you, Louisa. Perhaps you can help her accept the fact that Douglas is dead and put it behind her."

Louisa slouched on the sofa, her face pensive. "I'll try. I truly will. If I possibly can, I'll help Clara work through her loss of Douglas. It's devastating to lose the one you love. I'm finding out just how it feels." Louisa's face clouded as she stood up. "And I may need Clara to help me forget Peter McClough, Mother! He's shown himself to be irresponsible and inconsiderate!"

&

Jack Bradford's new assistant offered to take the family to the train depot the following Monday. Louisa extended her gloved hand as her father introduced the young man to his wife and daughter. Tall and broad-shouldered with dark hair and blue eyes, Roger Evans grasped Louisa's small hand in his larger one. The tanned face revealed a satisfied smile as his gaze swept over her figure and lingered. His direct approach, when he looked deeply into her eyes, left her blushing and unsure of herself. Louisa watched him closely as he loaded their luggage onto the carriage. He appeared rather handsome, she decided, and very sure of himself. His hair was not as dark as Peter's, but then neither was it as unruly. Roger's hair, slicked neatly into place, gave him a debonair appearance. And his brown suit, neatly pressed, looked perfect with highly polished brown shoes.

When Roger helped her into the carriage, she felt a warm sensation within her. Somewhat befuddled, Louisa murmured a low thank-you, blushed, and turned her eyes away. Roger grinned his self-satisfied grin and climbed into the driver's seat. Louisa wondered if the young man was married. Her father had offered no information about his new assistant, and she had not inquired. She'd been too taken up with her sadness over Peter's departure.

The short trip to the train station ended before she had

time to gather her thoughts. Roger Evans lifted her down with little effort and smiled as his blue eyes searched hers. "I'm glad I met you today, Louisa. I didn't know my boss had a daughter. He's kept you as a big, dark secret, and I can understand why. Lovely daughters need to be protected."

Louisa's face flushed, and she glanced away. Amused, Roger turned to Jack Bradford. "Have a safe trip," he said in his deep voice. "And don't worry about the bank, Jack. I'll take care of everything."

Jack Bradford extended his hand. "Thanks, Roger. I know the bank is in good hands. You have my brother's address if you need to get in touch."

"Good-bye," Roger said to the three of them. But his eyes lingered on Louisa.

Louisa and her parents settled into adjoining seats on the coach and relaxed. "Why haven't you told me about Roger, Father?" she asked eagerly. "He's quite handsome, isn't he? And he must be an able assistant for you to go off to Augusta for a week and leave him in charge. Is he married?"

"Uh, no, he isn't," Jack Bradford said absentmindedly. "But why are you interested? You are engaged to Peter, young lady. Have you forgotten?"

"No, Father, but Peter may be too undependable for me. Perhaps I was too hasty in accepting his ring. We may mutually agree to call the whole thing off. And if so, your assistant could be the one to help me forget Peter McClough."

"Louisa!" Elizabeth Bradford exclaimed. "You are so changeable! First you are in tears over Peter's departure and now you want to forget him. When you are in love with someone, you don't get over him so easily."

Louisa twisted in her seat and pulled some handwork out of her handbag. Memories of times shared with Peter flooded her mind, and she felt color rising in her cheeks. She did love him—or did she? No, she was angry with him. Maybe she still loved him. Maybe not. Sometimes she felt so confused she didn't understand her own feelings. Roger Evans, with his self-assured ways, could help her get over Peter. She glanced at her parents and sighed. They hadn't a care in the world. Jack Bradford read the morning paper, and her mother thumbed through a magazine.

"Your life is so settled, so happy, Mother. You and Father never had any problems in your relationship, did you?"

Elizabeth Bradford chuckled. "Of course we did, Louisa. All couples run up against problems. Your father and I had our share."

Louisa gasped in disbelief. "What happened? When did you have a problem? I can't remember a thing."

"Your father and I have had our differences of opinion through the years and still do. No two people always agree on everything. But that's a minor thing. It's a part of life. We work it out because we have God in our marriage to guide us. But we did have a large problem once."

"Tell me about it. I find it hard to believe you and Father ever had a big problem. Did it almost wreck your marriage?"

"We'd only been married about a year. I don't remember what the argument was about now, but it caused such stress I packed a valise and went home to my parents. You remember your grandparents' house, where they lived before their deaths. I was so angry I walked the few blocks in a very short time."

"What did Grandma and Grandpa say? Were they glad to have you back home?"

Jack Bradford glanced up from his newspaper and snorted. "No, they weren't! They told your mother to go home to her husband where she belonged."

Elizabeth Bradford giggled. "Your father was very upset, Louisa, and stubborn."

"Did they really tell you to go home to your husband?"

Elizabeth's face became serious. "Eventually they did. I was with them a few days and expected your father to come by and beg me to come back. He never came. His stubborn pride wouldn't allow it. Finally, my parents suggested I go home. As Christians, they reminded me God would not be pleased at our separation or a divorce. My place, as a Christian wife, was with my husband. I dishonored my wedding vows, 'Till death do us part,' by leaving your father over such a small matter."

"And you went home? Back to Father?"

"I went home and settled in. When your father came home from the bank that day, he was delighted to see me. He had been under a strain. We both realized how foolish we'd been. Our marriage could have ended before it had hardly gotten started. And you came to live with us shortly afterward. God blessed our home by allowing us to adopt you, a precious little girl."

"I. . .I almost can't believe it, Mother. You and Father quarreled over a small thing, enough to cause a separation. It seems impossible."

Jack Bradford folded his newspaper and eyed his daughter. "When young people get married, there is an adjustment. Your mother and I were very young. She was seventeen. I was nineteen. I worked at my father's bank back then. We needed some time to grow up. Being Christians from Christian homes helped. The entire episode made us realize we needed God in control of our lives in every situation." Jack Bradford patted his wife's arm and gave her an affectionate smile. "Your mother is a wonderful woman, Louisa."

"I know," Louisa said softly. "You are both very special people. Thanks for telling me about that part of your lives. It helps to know others have weathered storms and had victory over their problems. Life isn't a fairy tale or a smooth sailing trip like the books tell us. I've found that out during courtship with Peter. I wonder if I'm even marriage material."

"Of course you are, dear," Elizabeth Bradford said. "To the right man. . .at the right time."

Her mother's advice seemed so glib. Louisa already knew the pat answers, and they didn't satisfy her anxious feelings.

She picked up her handwork and worked quietly the balance of the trip. She had much to occupy her mind. Perhaps she and Peter could make a go of it. Or maybe God brought Roger Evans into her life for a purpose. He almost seemed too sure of himself. A very smooth character. His smile was captivating, and his eyes told her he was interested in her. But he could be interested in all young women—a playboy of sorts. She would have to be careful. Well, the week at her cousin Clara's home might solve some problems. Hopefully, Clara would come out of her shell and reenter the real world. She had been a recluse too long. And by chance Louisa would get over her anger toward Peter. Surely she would hear from him soon, and he would explain everything!

As the train pulled into the station in Augusta, Louisa questioned her parents. "Do Aunt Lydia, Uncle Phillip, and Clara know that I am adopted?"

"Lydia and Phillip know, dear," Elizabeth replied. They were with us when we got you. But they've never told Clara—didn't feel it necessary. You and Clara are as much cousins as if you were born to us. I don't think you could feel any closer than you do now."

❧

"Louisa! Am I glad to see you!" Clara Bradford exclaimed as she threw her arms around her cousin. Clara, a little taller than Louisa, had the same slight build. Her honey-colored hair, darker than Louisa's blond tresses, framed an oval face and hazel eyes. The two young ladies laughed and talked as they walked toward the waiting carriage. Both sets of parents followed them, talking rapidly.

"It's good to hear Clara laugh," Lydia Bradford said. "She's been such a moody person since she got word about Douglas's death. It's been several years since he was killed in the war. I know Louisa will be good for her. Listen to them. It's just like old times."

"Clara will be good for Louisa, also," Elizabeth Bradford

insisted. "Her fiancé, Peter McClough, left town abruptly without a word, and she is angry at him. Peter missed an appointment with her and hasn't written to explain."

"But your last letter said the wedding plans were almost settled," Lydia protested. "Are you saying it's all over between them?"

"I hope not. I'm praying this week will be a healing time for both of our girls."

six

"Annabelle!" Peter exclaimed. "Tell me what happened! Why did Thomas kill a man? I know he killed during the war. We all did. We had to follow orders. But this is different, isn't it? Did my brother actually kill someone after the war was over? Was he defending himself?"

Annabelle pursed her lips and looked at Peter through clouded eyes. She pushed back strands of loose, graying hair and tucked them into the bun at the nape of her neck. "This is a difficult story for me, Peter, but I'll spare you no details. I'm sure you've heard of the Ku Klux Klan. It was organized in May of last year in Nashville, Tennessee. They assembled to form an organization, an 'invisible empire,' against the blacks. Former Confederate General Nathan Bedford Forrest accepted the leadership as Grand Wizard of the Empire."

"I've heard of it, Annabelle. It's a secret terrorist society, isn't it? Tell me more about it."

"The secret Ku Klux Klan society wears white robes and masks with pointed hoods and terrorizes blacks by flogging and beating them. Sometimes they plant crosses on hillsides near the homes of those they hope to frighten. They have burned down the homes of some and have even instigated a number of lynchings."

Peter slammed his arm down on the table with a loud crash. "This is despicable! Where is the law? What is the reason for these terrible acts? Is my brother a member of this society, Annabelle? I have to know!"

"No, Thomas isn't a member. He abhors the society. The group justifies their actions as necessary in defense of what they call white supremacy. They aim to keep black folks from voting or holding office."

"If Thomas isn't a member of their group, why are you telling me about this?" Peter asked.

Annabelle sighed audibly, her eyes glazed with pain. "It all happened when Thomas left his plantation for a couple days. He hoped to locate some cattle and put in a bid for them. He and Ben had made a partnership. They fenced in several acres of pasture land. It was to be a co-ownership deal between the two men. Thomas felt it would be a profitable business for the two of them. Ben and his wife had two small children. Thomas was courting a young lady from a nearby plantation, someone he knew before the war. He planned to marry her but felt he needed to get financially stable first.

"When Thomas completed his business in Nashville, he started back to the plantation. The night was dark, and only a few stars dotted the heavens. As he neared his home, a huge fire lit the sky ahead of him. Thomas thought his barn was on fire. He galloped his mare at the highest possible speed and arrived in time to see several men in white sheets and pointed masks involved in a lynching."

Peter stared openmouthed, and Annabelle's voice caught in a little sob as she struggled to continue. "After the war, Thomas always carried his rifle at his side as he rode. It had become a habit with him. He wanted to be prepared in the event of danger. Thomas jumped from his horse, grabbed his rifle, and ran shouting toward the group of men. The blaze from the fire illuminated the face of the man hanging from the tree."

Peter pounded his right fist into his left hand, again and again. "It was Ben!" he shouted. "They murdered his friend! I know it was Ben!"

"Yes, it was Ben," Annabelle said quietly. "Thomas shouted at the group, but they galloped away toward the woods without a backward glance. Your brother took aim and fired. One of the horsemen fell. Thomas quickly took Ben down from the tree, but he was already dead. The fire raged through Ben's house. The structure tumbled to the ground before him, and Thomas could do nothing. Ben's wife and two little children died in the fire. Thomas's heart ached at the loss of his friends. He prepared a burial spot for them and went to check on the man he shot. The man lay face down, dead. So Thomas dragged his body to the burial spot and buried him, also. Thomas wept here in this room when he told me about the incident. Outraged and angry, he feared for his life. He had killed a man and would be wanted by the law. Thomas couldn't think straight. Instead of telling the authorities, he left early the next morning before sunup. He needed to get away from the place. Too many memories depressed him. Thomas and Ben owned four other horses, and they were safe in the barn. He brought them along and sold all four of them on his way north to see me last month. Depressed and agitated, he only stayed a few days. I'm worried about Thomas, Peter. He was so distraught."

"And you have no idea where he went? How can we help him if we don't know where he's gone? Thomas could be out of the country, Annabelle. Maybe he went into Canada. The underground railroad helped many escaped slaves reach Canada during the war. Would Thomas feel compelled to go there?"

Peter and his cousin continued to discuss some possible ideas of Thomas's whereabouts. They had no clues to go on, and after a light supper, Peter hooked up the team. He needed to get them back to the stable in town, but he promised Annabelle he would return the following day. Then they would discuss the situation further. Dusk fell quickly as he headed toward the outskirts of Boston. The horses trotted at a fast pace, anxious to get back to their stable and to bed down for the night. The rhythmic clip-clop, clip-clop of their hooves on the hard clay roadway had a soothing effect upon Peter. He watched the roads carefully as dusk settled around him. A wrong turn could delay his arrival back at the livery stable. His mind lingered on the many things he had gleaned from his cousin. It was rather overwhelming. The fact he had a brother had been good news. But his brother killed a man in Tennessee and fled the state. Would the law convict a man if they knew all the circumstances? Thomas was in trouble, and he and Annabelle wanted to help him. Could they even locate him? All these things preyed on his mind as he traveled the several miles back to Boston.

Peter guided the team and carriage down the side road leading to the livery stable. The young lad was not there, but an older man with gray hair helped Peter unhook the team.

"And how was yer day?" the older man asked. "Did the team suit yer needs? These are two of my finest horses and never give us any trouble." He patted their noble heads and led them toward their stalls in the barn. "Can we help you out again tomorrow with the same team?"

"They are a fine pair of horseflesh," Peter agreed, following the man into the stable. "They didn't give me a bit of trouble. But I've decided to buy a horse as I'll be around for a while. Do you have any horses for sale?"

The stable master showed him several available horses, and Peter selected a spirited black stallion with a white face. After riding him on a short jaunt, he paid the man and reserved the horse for the following day. "I'll pick him up in the morning, Sir, if that arrangement is agreeable with you."

The old stable master smiled. "You've made a good choice, young feller. I kinder hate to let Thunder go, but I have to think of my business. He's got too much spirit to pull a wagon or carriage. Some folks are afraid of him. Thunder likes to ride with the wind. I could see you were able to handle him. The two of you will make a fine pair."

Satisfied with his selection, Peter patted the horse's flanks and stroked the fine head. Then he walked briskly down the road toward the inn. He liked Thunder and the feel of the horse blended with his own body. They would make a good pair. He could travel to Annabelle's cottage quickly, and she had a small barn with stalls to house the animal. All the hay he needed could be purchased from the neighboring farm.

Peter undressed quickly and fell into bed. Exhausted from his busy day, he expected to fall asleep immediately. Instead, he lay wide-eyed and stared at the ceiling in the darkness. All the activities and discussions of the day controlled his mind and thoughts. Suddenly, he climbed out of bed and knelt beside it. "Lord, I don't know what to do about Thomas," he prayed aloud. "Somehow, I feel responsible for him since he's my brother. You alone know where he is and whether he plans to return to this area. Annabelle is so worried about him. Please give me wisdom and guidance, so I'll know what to do. I don't know where to begin, but I long to meet him. . . to know him. Thomas and Annabelle are the only family I have. And Lord, would You help Louisa understand about my absence? Let her know I would never disappoint her on purpose. I don't want to burden her with my problems—at least not yet. I love her, Lord, and believe marriage is in our future. Please keep her in Your care. She is very special to me. Thank You for all You've done for me already. In Jesus' name. Amen."

Rejuvenated from his prayer time, Peter stretched and yawned as he stood to his feet. He pushed back a shock of dark hair from his forehead and ran a hand across his eyes. They felt weary and bloodshot. A small light filtered through the window on the far side of the room. He walked toward it, pulled back the calico curtain, and gazed toward the heavens. The sky was dark, but the few visible stars twinkled. "God's up there in His wonderful Heaven," he whispered softly, "and He knows all about my problems. I'll just leave them with Him." Peter headed back toward his bed with a broad grin on his face. He felt God's presence and His peace. "Now, I can sleep!" he said. And he did.

seven

"Let's go shopping, Clara," Louisa said eagerly, in an attempt to get her cousin out of the house. Louisa and her parents had been visiting the Phil Bradfords in Augusta for almost a week. Louisa had tried in vain to interest her cousin in some semblance of a social life. She and Clara sat in the parlor while they worked dutifully on embroidery and other handwork.

"We must leave in a few days to go back to Waterville, and I've not had much opportunity to see the town," Louisa said as she placed her handwork on the sofa next to her. She stood up, stretched, and patted her pale, gold hair which fell in a cascade about her shoulders. "I'm bored with handwork. We need to get some excitement into our lives."

Clara grimaced. "Like what, dear cousin? I'm content to work on my pillowcases and dream thoughts of Douglas. We would have been married by this time and perhaps had a child. Why did that terrible war happen anyway? It ruined so many lives."

Louisa grabbed Clara's handwork from her cousin's lap and pulled her to her feet. "I've been patient with you long enough, young lady. It's a lovely day, and we need some fresh air. We are going out on the town!"

The Phil Bradford home, a large brownstone house just off the main street, was in close proximity to many interesting shops. Louisa felt the outing and exercise would do them both good. Since their arrival in Augusta, the only place they had visited was the church. It was bigger than their church in Waterville, but the people seemed friendly, and the pastor preached the Word of God. One gentleman in particular seemed very attentive to Clara. He talked to them at great length after the morning service.

"Doesn't Sam Burns work at the pharmacy?" Louisa asked, referring to the young man from church. "Let's stop by and see him when we're out."

Clara eyed her cousin carefully. "Why, Louisa? Do you find Sam attractive?"

Louisa blushed under Clara's scrutiny. "Why yes, I do. Don't you think Sam is handsome? He has such broad shoulders and a manly build."

"Not to mention his blue eyes and sandy-colored hair." Clara laughed. "I'd say you were over Peter McClough, cousin, if you can find another interest so quickly."

"I'm interested in Sam for you, Clara. I saw his attentiveness to you in church. Didn't you see the way he watched you? That young man is in love with you, or close to it."

"Fiddle!" Clara exclaimed. "He's just being friendly. Sam was Douglas's best friend. The two men did everything together. . .played sports, went fishing and hunting. They went off to war and were in the same unit. Sam came back wounded. Douglas was killed. It all happened in the same battle." Clara pulled her lace handkerchief from her bodice and dabbed at her eyes.

"Do you hold that against Sam?"

"What. . .what do you mean?" Clara stammered.

"Sam came back, and Douglas didn't. Do you think it's unfair for Sam to be alive? Is this the reason you can't recognize that the man loves you?"

"Nonsense!" Clara said, blowing her nose.

Louisa put an arm around her cousin. "I'm sorry, Clara, I didn't mean to upset you. Dry your eyes, and we'll go to town. You need to get out of this house!"

After a light lunch with their parents, the two cousins, decked with bonnets and parasols, started for town. Phil Bradford took some days off work at his bank so the two brothers and their wives could visit. Other days Jack Bradford accompanied his brother to his bank while the womenfolk busied themselves at the house.

The sun shone brightly upon the girls as they walked uptown. Clara, quiet at first, relaxed under Louisa's constant chatter. "Oh, look, a millinery shop!" Louisa squealed. "Let's go in and try on hats!"

Louisa's excitement caught on, and the two entered the shop with enthusiasm. A nice-looking middle-aged woman approached them with a smile and nodded at Clara. "Hello Clara. What can I do for you young ladies? Is it time for a new bonnet?"

"My cousin, Louisa Bradford, is visiting from Waterville, Miss Martin. We would like to try on some hats."

"Of course. Nice to meet you, Louisa. Just help yourself and let me know if you find something you like. I have another lady trying on hats at the moment."

Louisa and Clara settled themselves by a mirror and selected several hats to try on. They giggled and laughed at some outrageous ones, overdone with extravagant plumes, artificial birds, and flowers. Louisa watched her cousin with amusement. Clara was definitely coming out of her shell. They looked across the room and saw a somewhat sophisticated, tall, thin woman trying on hats. Each hat she chose was tall and thin like herself. Louisa and Clara had a difficult time as they struggled to control their laughter. "Why do tall, thin people pick tall, thin hats?" Clara whispered as she giggled quietly. Presently the woman purchased her hat and left the store.

The bell on the millinery shop door tinkled merrily as another customer entered. This lady was short and stout with several packages in her arms. She plopped herself into a chair on the far side of the room, and Miss Martin hurried to wait on her. All the hats Miss Martin brought she refused to try on. They were stylish and complemented the lady's figure and coloring. "No! No! No!" she insisted. "They are all too tall for me, Miss Martin." Instead, she chose a small round hat—one which matched her well-rounded body and did nothing to enhance her appearance.

"Did you see the hat she chose?" Clara asked quietly as she suppressed her giggles with her hand. "Why didn't she take Miss Martin's suggestion?"

"It would have been a much better selection, indeed," Louisa agreed with a smile as she placed a large wide-brimmed hat on her golden head. "I like this, Clara. What do you think?"

"It's lovely. I like the pink flowers and ribbons. It becomes you."

"Are you sure? It isn't too wild, is it? I probably don't need a new hat, but this one is different. I brought enough money with me to purchase it. This is the kind of hat I've always wanted. It will lift my spirits and help me forget Peter."

Louisa made her decision and purchased the hat before she could change her mind. An elderly lady, who entered the store while they were still at the counter, tried on a brilliantly deep pink hat, complete with plumes and feathers. It fit nicely over the gray hair piled high upon her head. "Tell me, girls," she called to them. "Am I too old for this kind of hat? Miss Martin says it makes me look younger."

Clara and Louisa turned to face the elderly woman. The deep pink of the hat brought color out in the sunken cheeks and added a glow to the dark eyes.

"I like it!" Clara said. "Miss Martin is right. It makes you look younger. I'm sure heads will turn when they see you in it."

"Yes, indeed!" Louisa agreed. "The hat is very becoming. I think you will be happy with your purchase."

"Thank you, young ladies," the elderly woman said. "I've had my eye on this hat for a long while. It's been in the window enticing me each time I went by the shop. I just needed enough nerve to come in and buy it. I always appreciate an outside opinion." She turned to Miss Martin and smiled a mischievous smile. "Wrap it up! I can't wait until my husband sees me in this!"

Louisa and Clara walked leisurely down the main street and entered a few other shops. They purchased some new needles, embroidery thread, and ribbon at the variety store. When they came to the corner pharmacy, Louisa turned to go in.

"You were serious about visiting Sam, weren't you?" Clara asked as she followed her cousin. "Won't he think we're being a little forward?"

"I don't think so. I can purchase some small item if it makes you feel more comfortable. Sam will probably be delighted to see us."

The two cousins walked around the pharmacy and noticed Sam with a customer at the far end of the store. It was a young woman who giggled and gushed as she talked with him. Louisa and Clara busied themselves as they looked at the many items for sale, going from one aisle to another. Suddenly a deep, resonant voice behind them broke into their thoughts.

"Good afternoon Clara, Louisa. How are you young ladies today? It's good to see you. May I assist you with something?"

The two cousins turned simultaneously. Clara's face turned dark crimson as she faced Sam. "Uh, no, thank you, Sam. We were just looking around."

Sam reached for her hand and held it briefly. "I see by your packages you and Louisa have been shopping. Isn't it a beautiful day?"

"It is a beautiful day, and we've enjoyed the walk and fresh air," Louisa said. She noticed Clara seemed at a loss for words. "Clara helped me select a new hat to take back to Waterville with me. It's somewhat daring, but it seems to lift my spirits."

"I'm sure it's a lovely bonnet," Sam said, "especially if Clara liked it. I've noticed she has impeccable taste in clothing and hats."

Sam's green eyes lingered on Clara's honey-blond hair and hazel-gray eyes as he spoke. She continued to blush, averting her eyes from his constant gaze. When she replied, it was with great effort. "Thank you, Sam, but I'm sure you are just being kind."

"I have a great idea," Sam said with a quick smile. "There is a concert next Friday at the Theatre House. Would you young ladies allow me the privilege of escorting you? It would give me great pleasure."

Clara stood quietly as though struggling for words.

"Thank you very much," Louisa said, breaking the silence. "But I cannot accept your generous offer. Our family is returning to Waterville in a few days. However, I'm sure Clara would enjoy going to the concert with you."

Sam's ruddy face broke into a wide grin. "Would you, Clara? Will you consider going to the concert with me?"

Clara hesitated as she glanced at her cousin and then at Sam. Why had Louisa put her cousin in this predicament? It would be rude for her to decline. "Uh, yes, Sam," she murmured breathlessly "I'll go to the concert with you next week. Thank you for your kind invitation."

Louisa saw the look of pleasure that covered Sam's face at Clara's answer. What a fine and handsome young man he was! She hoped this was the start of a lasting relationship between them. It gave her a happy feeling to know Clara and Sam planned to attend the concert together. They would make a fine couple, and her instincts told her Sam could help Clara get over Douglas. She detected a certain magnetism between them.

When the girls left the pharmacy, they decided to stop at the nearby cafe for tea. Clara seemed unusually quiet, and Louisa hesitated to break into her thoughts. Finally, when they were settled with their tea, she reached out and patted her cousin's hand. "Clara, are you angry at me? I know I made it impossible for you to refuse Sam's invitation. I'm sorry if I've offended you. But I thought an evening at the concert would be a good change. You spend too much of your time at home with your handwork."

Clara remained silent and took small sips of her tea. She tucked a strand of dark, gold hair back into her bonnet with her free hand. A few ringlets lingered about her fair cheeks, and her eyes were moist.

"Dear Clara, I'm so sorry!" Louisa exclaimed. "I've been such a fool! I forced you into an awkward situation you couldn't refuse. Please forgive me. I've been a meddling cousin and caused you unnecessary heartache."

Clara wiped her moist eyes with her lace handkerchief. "There's nothing to forgive, Louisa. I'm glad you meddled. It's time I accepted an invitation from Sam. He's invited me several times before, but I always refused. When I look at Sam, I see Douglas by his side. They were always a pair. When Douglas courted me before the war, Sam came along sometimes. . .on picnics or to church outings. I knew Sam was interested in me back then. It made me feel special. But he was always the gentleman. He never tried to move in on Doug's territory, and he seemed happy for the two of us. Sam was to be best man at our wedding."

"Will it be too difficult to be courted by Doug's best friend? I didn't realize the whole situation when I got you into this."

Clara smiled. "Actually, I'm looking forward to next week with Sam. He lost his best friend in the war. I lost my sweetheart. And Sam has been very patient with me. I can't expect him to wait around forever."

"Don't you think Douglas would be happy if his two favorite people got together, Clara? It almost seems like it was meant to be."

Clara toyed with her napkin. "Douglas wrote to me from the battlefield. He told me once, if anything happened to him in the war, he wanted me to consider Sam as a future husband.

He believed Sam to be the finest friend a man could have on this earth. You see, Doug knew how much Sam cared for me. He also knew Sam would never attempt to court me while Doug was in the picture. I've kept all Doug's letters and reread them recently."

"Well, you certainly have Doug's blessing on a relationship with Sam through his letters, Clara. Sam cares deeply for you. It's evident in the way he looks at you. He seems such a fine person. Do you think you will ever grow to love him?"

Louisa was surprised at Clara's answer. "I think I've always loved him as a good friend. And today, for the first time, I felt the liberty to love him in a deeper way. Doug gave me that liberty through his letters, and you gave me courage to accept his invitation to the concert next week. Thank you, Louisa. I thought it was my duty to be faithful to Doug's memory and remain unmarried, but I see things differently now. I feel like a caged bird who has just been set free. It is the Lord's doing, and I praise Him for it."

eight

The week's visit with the Phillip Bradford family ended on a happy note. When Louisa bid Clara good-bye, her cousin bubbled with excitement. She no longer dwelt on the past but eagerly looked forward to the future. "I wouldn't be a bit surprised," Louisa told her, "if we receive a letter soon announcing your upcoming marriage."

"Louisa! Do you really think so? But it's too soon. We've not begun our courtship yet. Sam and I may find we are not compatible."

"No chance of that!" Louisa insisted. "Now that you are over Douglas, everything will fall into place. You are over him, aren't you?"

"I still have wonderful memories of my relationship with Doug, but I accept the fact he is gone. Sam Burns fills my thoughts and dreams now." Clara hugged her cousin. "You've been so good for me, Louisa. You are looking at the new Clara Bradford. I hope you and Peter get married when he gets back. You spoke so highly of him in your letters. I want you to be as happy as I am."

Louisa smiled wistfully. "I thought I would be the one getting married soon. I must admit I'm a little envious, Clara. When Sam looks at you, I see the love in his eyes. And actually you've known him a long time. It isn't as though you just met. I've known Peter a long time, also, but it seems he has tired of me. Perhaps I've taken our relationship too much for granted."

"Fiddlesticks!" Clara exclaimed. "You'll probably have a letter waiting when you get home which explains his absence. Or maybe Peter will be there in person. Wouldn't that be grand?"

Louisa smiled ruefully at her cousin's exuberance. "I

might, Clara, and thanks for the encouragement. However, I'm so angry at Peter I'm not even sure I want to see him "

Louisa worked dutifully on her handwork during the train trip home. Her parents dozed or read the morning paper, and she tried to keep her mind occupied between her embroidery and the scenery. But her thoughts constantly turned to Peter McClough and his whereabouts. *Perhaps there will be a letter waiting when I return home as Clara suggested. Or Peter might be there in person to explain his sudden departure. But why would he leave so suddenly without a word? Was it something in his past? Something he was ashamed to tell me?* She felt concerned about Peter one moment and angry the next. *What if some harm has come to him? Could he have discovered a serious illness and gone to seek professional treatment not available in Waterville? Doesn't he realize I care about him and want to know what is going on in his life? I miss the closeness we shared. His dark eyes searching mine spoke of his love. I remember sweet and tender kisses as he bid me good-bye after an evening at the concert or a dinner engagement. A lock of his dark, unruly hair always fell across his forehead. I loved to push it back as I studied his firm jaw and wide grin. How I long to feel his strong arms around me once again. Oh, Peter, why don't you contact me? Whatever your burden may be, I want to share it with you.* The next moment her mood changed completely. *Peter McClough evidently doesn't care enough about me to share his secret. He is thoughtless and inconsiderate! If there is someone else, someone from his past, he should have told me. If I cannot come first in his life, there is no hope for us.*

As the Bradford family stepped down from the train in Waterville, Louisa spied Roger Evans waiting with the Bradfords' team and carriage. Jack Bradford had arranged earlier for Roger to meet their train and care for the team during their absence. Louisa noticed Roger's tall, muscular body and self-assured stance. He looked very debonair in a dark suit and tie as he approached the trio with a dazzling smile.

"How was your trip?" he asked.

"Fine, Roger," Jack Bradford replied. "How are things at the bank? Any problems I should know about?"

"Everything is in good shape at the bank, Sir. I've handled everything. I'm sure you will be pleased."

Louisa detected a note of inflated ego, but the young man's smile pushed the thought aside. His next words took her by surprise.

"Mr. Bradford, may I escort your daughter to the concert at the music hall next week? It should be a most enjoyable evening, especially if Louisa could attend with me."

Jack Bradford studied the young man for a moment. "She is engaged to be married, Roger. I'm sure you didn't know."

"I didn't know the circumstances, Sir. I suppose the concert is out of the question then." Roger Evans turned toward Louisa, and his gaze lingered as he took in her appearance. She wore a deep mauve traveling outfit along with her newly purchased hat. The ensemble brought out the gold of her hair and enhanced her fair coloring. "Who is the lucky fellow, Louisa, and when is the wedding?"

Color rose in Louisa's cheeks. "His name is Peter Mc-Clough. We planned to marry this fall, but Peter left town suddenly. I'm not sure where he is or when he will be back."

Roger Evans cleared his throat. "That sounds unusual for an engaged man to go off somewhere and not tell his betrothed. Is there a possibility things may not work out? A broken engagement maybe?"

Louisa's cheeks felt hot as the color rose higher under his careful gaze and self-assured smile. She felt his eyes penetrating her very being. "I do not know, Mr. Evans," she said as she climbed into the carriage. "Only time will tell."

Roger Evans loaded the Bradfords' luggage and headed the carriage down Main Street. Louisa's thoughts centered around Roger during the short ride to the Bradford home. He seemed nice enough, she decided, but his self-confident manner took her off guard. He made it clear he would be interested in her if she broke off her engagement. Would she do that in the near future if there was no word from Peter? She mulled it over and over in her mind but was unable to arrive at a suitable conclusion.

There was no letter from Peter when Jack Bradford picked up the family mail the following day—nor was there any sign of his return. Louisa tried to give Peter the benefit of the doubt but grew more and more impatient with the passing of time. "I will blot Peter McClough out of my life!" she declared aloud in her room one afternoon. "He is not worth all my worry and concern! I'll show him I can get along fine without him! Roger Evans appears to be much more of a gentleman anyway. If he asks me out again, I may accept his invitation!"

Later that week Louisa stopped in at the bank and visited briefly with Roger Evans while there. He invited her again to attend a concert with him, strictly as a friend, since he knew she was engaged. "Since Peter is out of town, surely he wouldn't mind you attending a concert with a friend," Roger suggested. "You need to have a social life."

"I don't know. . .I'm not sure," she murmured. "It probably wouldn't be proper."

"Think of me simply as your father's business associate, Louisa. It will simply be a friendly evening out for both of us."

Louisa hemmed and hawed a bit, but finally agreed—on a strictly friendly basis—nothing more. When her parents learned she planned to attend a concert with Roger Evans, they were dumbfounded and strongly advised against it. But Louisa held her ground and said there was no harm in it since it was just two friends who enjoyed music spending a little time together.

As Louisa dressed for the concert, she determined to look her best and enjoy the evening to the fullest. Deftly, she pulled out one gown after another and tossed them on the bed. Not the blue satin, she decided. It was Peter's favorite. He always said it made her gray eyes light up with glints of blue. She held up the cranberry velvet but discarded it quickly. Another of Peter's favorites, it was more appropriate for the winter season. Finally her decision fell on the light pink satin gown with lace, brocade trim, and tiny pink roses sewed onto the formfitting bodice. She grimaced as she viewed herself in the mirror and sighed. "Peter loves this dress also. He says it brings out the pale gold of my hair." Suddenly she cried out furiously, "Stop it Louisa! Don't concern yourself with what Peter likes or dislikes. He isn't here, nor has he contacted me. Think instead about a casual but interesting evening with a friend. And that is all there is to it!"

Roger Evans arrived at the Bradford home promptly at seven on the Friday evening of the concert. He wore a black suit and his dark hair was slicked back from his broad forehead. When Louisa descended the staircase in her pink satin gown, Roger rushed to greet her. "How beautiful you look, Louisa," he said with glints of admiration in his blue eyes. "I'll be the envy of every man at the concert."

Louisa smiled and extended her hand, while hints of color tinged her cheeks. She felt a little guilty but dismissed the thought immediately. "Thank you, kind Sir," she said demurely. "You look mighty fine, yourself."

"There's a chill in the night air," Roger said as he helped Louisa pull her warm cloak around her shoulders. A hood fell loosely at the back, and he pulled the hood forward to cover the golden curls. "That hood will keep you warm and cozy."

The concert proved to be one of the better ones. The soprano, tenor, and baritone sang beautiful arias, sometimes together and sometimes interchangeably. Louisa felt herself being lifted to a higher plane of music appreciation as she listened wide-eyed with lips parted. "It's so lovely," she whispered to Roger. He leaned over, placed his arm around the back of her seat, and rested it on her shoulders. Louisa moved away slightly, but he only moved closer. His arm on her shoulder seemed too familiar, and his closeness unnerved her. She leaned forward in her seat and pushed his arm away with a smile. "Remember our agreement, Roger," she whispered, "this is just a little outing between two friends."

"Um. . .yes, it is." Roger's face registered disappointment, and he shifted in his seat. "But you are so lovely, my dear." His breath, warm and heavy on her ear, was too close for comfort.

During intermission Louisa excused herself to go to the powder room. As she glanced into the mirror, she noticed hot pink spots lingered on her cheeks. She fussed with her hair and tucked some stray ringlets behind her ears. Satisfied with her appearance, she turned to go. On her way out, a very attractive brunette, draped in blue brocade, approached.

"Isn't it a lovely concert?" the dark-haired woman gushed.

"Yes," Louisa agreed, "I've enjoyed it very much."

The young woman eyed Louisa up and down. "I see you are attending with Roger Evans. Isn't he dashing? He seems to be quite the man about town, doesn't he?"

"I. . .I wouldn't know," Louisa faltered. "I've not known him very long. We're just casual friends. I think he's only been in town a few weeks."

"Where have you been hiding, dearie? He's squired many women in the short time he's been here. I was one of his first. I still see him now and then. He seems to want variety and moves around rather fast."

Louisa frowned. The woman's chatter had a nauseating effect on her. "Please excuse me, Miss. This discussion is of no interest to me." She deliberately passed around the young woman and headed out of the powder room door.

"Well, I never!" the woman exclaimed.

Louisa's skirts rustled as she hurried back down the aisle, the frown still on her face.

"What is it?" Roger asked as he stood to greet her. "You look angry about something."

Her face relaxed into a slight smile. "I met someone in the powder room who was not very pleasant. It's nothing to worry about. I've put it out of my mind already."

Roger pulled her down into the seat next to him but kept his distance. "Good. We don't want anything to mar this evening. And your pretty face looks so much better when you smile." He leaned close and whispered in her ear. "I'd rather watch you than the performers any day!"

When Roger took her home, he walked her to the door and boldly leaned to kiss her good night. Louisa, taken by surprise, pushed him from her. She couldn't deny the warm feelings she felt for this man, but she disliked the liberties he took with her person.

"Is something wrong?" Roger asked. "It was only intended to be a friendly kiss. Did I offend you?"

"No. . .yes!" Louisa faltered. "I mean, I'm engaged! Friendship does not include kisses. Besides, we hardly know one another."

Roger studied the uplifted face before him. "I intend to change that, Louisa." He looked deep into her eyes. "If Peter McClough doesn't return to claim his bride, I shall do my best to steal you away from him!"

Louisa felt warm inside and turned away. "Thank you for a lovely evening, Roger. It will take some time for us to get better acquainted. . .as friends. I don't know very much about you, your background, or your family. My life is an open book. You've met my parents. I've always lived in Waterville. There's not much else to know."

"You're sweet, Louisa. I admire your shyness. May I take you to dinner next week or call on you sometime soon?" he asked eagerly. "We need to spend a lot of time together. I can fill you in on my background if you wish. It's not very exciting."

"Would you like to attend church with our family on Sunday?" Louisa asked. "We attend the little Community Church here in town."

"Church?" Roger asked, taken aback. "I. . .I guess so. Why

not? Especially if it will please you."

"Are you not in the habit of attending church on the Lord's Day?" Louisa asked. "The Bible instructs us to assemble ourselves together. I'm a Christian, Roger, and attending services is part of my life. What are your feelings toward God?"

Roger rubbed his chin as he thought for a moment. He realized this question was important to the young woman standing before him. "I believe there is a God up there somewhere. I just don't think about it much. I guess I'm a Christian, too."

"Christian means 'little Christ.' The only way one becomes a Christian is by trusting Jesus Christ, God's Son, as their Savior. Have you ever done that, Roger?"

"I think so, as a young lad. I can't remember for sure. My grandmother talked to me about it once. And I'll visit your church if you like. I'm sure it will be good for me."

As Louisa undressed for bed, her thoughts dwelt on Roger Evans. He was a bold one—but also very charming. She felt guilty about the warm glow she felt when she was with him. It seemed obvious he didn't know God in a personal way. But neither did Peter at first, and his life changed when he came to know Jesus. The same thing could happen to Roger, she reasoned. Louisa walked to the window and gazed out at the heavens. One star shone brightly and twinkled at her. "Star light, star bright. . . ," she started, then stopped. "Oh I don't know what my wish would be if I could have one. *Help me, dear God. Is Roger Evans just a playboy as that woman suggested at the concert tonight? And what about Peter? Where is he and what is happening to him?*"

Louisa knelt quietly by her bed and poured out her heart before God. Did she err by attending a concert with Roger Evans—on a strictly friendly basis on her part? He hinted that he would like their relationship to be something more than friends. Perhaps it could be so, if Peter never returned. She didn't have any answers, but she knew the great God of the universe was in complete control.

nine

Peter had settled into his brother's old room at Annabelle's cottage. It had two cotlike beds and a single dresser. A small window with calico curtains which matched the bedspread completed the decor. It was homey and comfortable. Somehow it reached out to Peter and reminded him of the brother he had never known. Thomas had slept there, used the dresser for his clothes, and looked out the window. He could almost feel his presence.

His mother's cousin, due to her age, seemed more an aunt than a distant cousin to him. She hovered over him and cooked all his favorite meals—delighted to have someone to wait on. There had been no word from Thomas, and Annabelle grew more concerned as time went by. Peter busied himself around the cottage and outbuildings. He fixed the roof and made other needed repairs to the small home. When he mended the fences of the pasture, his horse Thunder followed him from place to place. The animal seemed to enjoy his new surroundings and showed his appreciation by nudging his new master. Peter rode the spirited animal at least once a day around the pasture or down the lane. It was the high point of his day as the two of them, the man and his stallion, blended as one and galloped across the valley at a magnificent pace. The high speed left Peter with a tremendous feeling of exultation and accomplishment. During these rides, Peter put his brother's problems out of his mind and thought only about Louisa. How he longed to see her and hold her in his arms. "I love you, Louisa!" he shouted to the wind. "I love you!"

When they returned to the barn, the beautiful animal

panted and pawed at the ground. Peter, breathless and exuberant, jumped off his horse and removed the saddle and reins. He led Thunder to his stall where he rubbed him down and brushed his black coat until it shone. Thunder nuzzled his master, and Peter patted his head letting his fingers run through the thick black mane. "What a beautiful animal you are. And you're hungry, aren't you, fella?" He reached for the pitchfork, went over to a mound of hay, and tossed hay into the stall. Thunder jerked his head up and down and quickly grabbed a mouthful of the feed. Deep in thought, Peter watched his horse munch quietly for a few moments before leaving the barn.

By the time he chopped some wood and carried water into the house, it was time for supper. After washing up, he sat down at the table and took a deep breath. The sumptuous odors coming from the wood stove filled his nostrils. "Annabelle, what smells so good? I'm so hungry, I could eat my hat!"

Annabelle chuckled as she carried an iron pot of stew from the wood stove to the table. "Just stew and dumplings, my boy. It does my heart good to cook for someone who so thoroughly enjoys my cooking."

After the hearty meal, complete with blueberry pie, Peter leaned back and patted his stomach. "Annabelle, I'm getting fat. It's your wonderful home cooking. I'm afraid I'll resemble one of your neighbor's pigs if I don't watch myself."

Annabelle's merry little laugh tinkled forth. "Peter, you can't know how much it means to me having you here." Her face grew serious. "I worry so about Thomas. What will happen to him because he killed a man?" She shuddered as she spoke. "If he would only come back, we could work out a plan. Do you think he will have to pay for his crime?"

Peter frowned. "I don't know, Annabelle. But I've done a lot of thinking lately. Thomas might stay away until he thinks the episode has blown over. But who knows how long that will take? I can't wait any longer. I've decided to go to

Tennessee and find out more about this incident. Maybe Thomas went back there and turned himself in. Do you think it's a possibility?"

Annabelle stared straight ahead, her face downcast. "I don't know, Peter. It is possible. He was in a terrible state when he left here. I just don't know what to think. It frightens me to think about it. Would. . ." Her voice faltered. "Would they hang him for his crime?"

Peter shoved back his chair and jumped up, a sick feeling in the pit of his stomach. "I can't sit around and do nothing! This matter needs to be dealt with! I'll leave early tomorrow morning for Tennessee. Try not to fret about it, Annabelle."

"When will you return?" she asked. "Could I go with you?"

"No, Annabelle. I'm not sure what I'll find or how long it will take. I'll need an address and directions to the Berringer Plantation. Can you help me with that?"

"I have an address, and I know it's north of Nashville. If you go into town, someone will know the location."

"What name does my brother go by? Is he called Thomas Berringer, the name of his foster parents? Or does he carry your last name, Annabelle? It will help to know who I'm looking for."

"It pleased me to know he called himself Thomas Hayes when he joined the Confederates. When I wrote him in the army, I sent my letters to that name."

"Good!" Peter exclaimed giving his cousin a little hug. "Then I'll search for news about Thomas Hayes, who happens to be my brother."

"God go with you, Peter," Annabelle whispered softly.

At first light on the following day, Peter saddled Thunder, tied his belongings to the back of his saddle, and headed toward Boston. Dark clouds dotted the horizon, and soft drops of rain dripped from his hat as Thunder raced toward town. He wasn't sure when he would see his lovely Louisa again, but he knew the task before him must take priority. It would consume his mind and energy for a time. When he resolved the situation with his brother, Peter planned to return to Waterville. Would Louisa wait for him? He prayed she would. His heart thudded inside his chest as he rode to the train station and purchased a ticket to Nashville.

For a small fee, the ticket master allowed Thunder to bed down in one of the empty freight cars. Peter tethered the animal, bought some hay and straw from the man at the livery stable, and made the freight car comfortable for his faithful charge.

As the train raced toward his final destination, Peter organized a plan in his mind. He would visit the town and casually inquire about the Berringer Plantation. Surely someone could provide him with sufficient information—perhaps even the details of the tragic event. It must be done tactfully, he decided, especially since he was from the North. His speech would betray him immediately. He knew many Southerners carried a deep resentment toward Northerners, and it was understandable. The war, tragic to both sides, left the South ravished in many areas. They lost husbands, sons, and other loved ones in bloody battles just as the North did. But many wealthy Southern folk also lost their homes and very existence. The cotton industry was their livelihood on the large plantations. With slaves set free, they had no one to work the cotton fields and care for their animals. Plantation owners faced a tremendous loss and difficult time as they strove to get their lives back together again.

Peter leaned back and tried to sleep. "I'm not certain what kind of a reception to expect in Nashville," he muttered to himself. "They may run this Northerner out of town—or tar and feather me." With eyes closed, a slight smile curved his lips. "Now wouldn't that be a sight to behold! Peter McClough, what are you letting yourself in for, anyway?"

When the train finally arrived in Nashville two days later, Peter grabbed his belongings and went to the freight car to get Thunder. The horse whinnied at the sight of his master, snorted and pranced, nodding his fine head. Peter removed the tether which held Thunder secure and examined the animal carefully. He seemed none the worse for wear.

Peter led him out of the freight car, saddled up, and swung his long legs over Thunder's sleek, black body. The horse, eager to run, started off at a rapid pace.

"Whoa, boy!" Peter shouted, as he reined in the animal to a slow walk. "We're in town, not out in the pasture. I know you're anxious to run, fella, and we'll do that later. We need to mosey down the road first and get some information."

Peter noticed an attractive young woman watching him with a big smile on her face. She fluttered her fan back and forth and peered at him with violet eyes. "Do you always talk to your horse, Sir?" she asked in a soft and delightful Southern drawl. "Is it just your way or do all Northerners talk to their animals?"

Peter grinned as he reined Thunder to a stop. "I'm afraid my conversation gave me away already," he replied. "I don't know about all Northerners, but I like to talk to my animal. He's my friend."

As if he knew what his master said, Thunder nickered and jerked his head up and down. "Well, I can see your animal knows he's your friend. Good day to you, Sir."

"Wait, Miss. Can you give me directions to the Berringer Plantation? I understand it's north of the city a small piece."

The young lady's face turned ashen, and she clutched at her throat. "Why do you ask, Sir? Do you have business there?"

Peter quickly jumped down from Thunder's back. "Did I say something to disturb you, Miss?"

"I. . .ah. . .no!" she exclaimed. "It's really none of my affair." She turned on her heel and started away. Her lovely yellow dress rustled as she moved quickly toward the town.

Peter hurried after her and blocked her way. "I'm sorry,

Miss. I'm not familiar with Nashville. Can you tell me the road that leads to the Berringer place? That's all I ask."

"Sir, you are blocking my path!" she said. Hot pink patches stood out on her fair cheeks, and her violet eyes displayed fire. "Ask at the ticket office," she flung over her shoulder as she marched away, her chestnut hair bouncing under her bonnet. "Or ask the sheriff over at the jailhouse. I'm sure he'd like to know about your interest in the Berringer place."

Peter watched the slight figure as she continued down the roadway. "Thanks, I will!" he called after her. But she did not look back.

The ticket master was closest, so Peter turned Thunder around and retreated to the train station. The ticket master studied a schedule, but glanced up as Peter approached. When he asked for directions to the Berringer Plantation, the man's eyes narrowed. He looked Peter up and down several times before answering. "What's yer business here, mister?" he asked. "We don't cotton to Northerners in our parts. You'd best get back up north where you belong."

Peter flashed his friendliest smile. "I don't plan to stay in Nashville, Sir. I'm only here for a short time, and I'll be on my way north. Could you tell me which road to take out of town and about how far it is to Berringers'?"

"The place is deserted, mister. Are you interested in buying the place? Old man Berringer and his wife are both dead. Their only daughter married and moved away a few years ago."

"Wasn't there a foster son?" Peter asked, trying to sound nonchalant. "I heard he fought for the South in the War Between the States."

The man's eyes narrowed into tiny slits and his lips formed a tight line. Deep frown lines furrowed the wide forehead. "Take the main road through town all the way to the end. There's a road that winds north. . .can't miss it. The Berringer place is about three miles out on the left-hand side. It's a large, white house with pillars and sits back a piece from the road."

The ticket master abruptly turned his back on Peter and moved to another part of the room.

"Thank you, Sir," Peter called after him. "I appreciate your help."

Peter swung himself into the saddle once again and headed Thunder toward the town's main street. It was still early in the day, and he decided to ride out and see the plantation before dark. As the horse trotted through town, Peter noticed a small cafe on one corner and an inn on the other. Several horses were tied to the hitching post at the cafe, and throngs of people milled about on the roadway. "Must be good food there, Thunder. That's where I'll eat later and then stay overnight at the inn. We'll find a livery stable for you with lots of good hay and oats." He patted the animal's neck as he leaned over him. "As soon as we're out of town, we'll ride with the wind!"

It was not difficult to locate the Berringer Plantation, a magnificent antebellum estate, white with large pillars, set back from the main road boasting of better days. An iron gate opened to a tree-lined roadway which led to the house. As far as Peter could see from the outside, the home was in good repair just as Annabelle said. His brother, Thomas, and friend, Ben, had taken care of all the renovations after the war. The home was locked, but Peter peeked through some windows and caught glimpses of beautiful furnishings. "This is quite the mansion!" he exclaimed, letting out a low whistle. "My brother has a fortune tied up in this place!"

Peter moved cautiously about the grounds. He examined the barn, which was also in excellent repair. The stalls were clean and well taken care of. Pasture and cotton fields extended as far as his eyes could see. At the back and off to one side, Peter came upon the rubble left from Ben's home. It was reduced to a pile of burnt boards in memory of the wife and two children who died there. Peter removed his hat and bowed his head. Farther back he stumbled upon the graves.

Thomas had dug them hastily but carefully. Boards nailed together in the form of a cross stood by each grave. Somehow Thomas had managed to write their names, evidently burning the letters into the wood. Peter felt pain and despair wash over him as he read the names: Ben, my best friend; Lily, his wife; Ben Jr.; and, lastly, Liza. One other grave had a huge empty hole. It had evidently been dug up and the body removed to another site. A wooden cross with no name stood by the empty grave. *This was the burial spot of the man Thomas killed in an angry rage. His family must have removed him to their own burial grounds. Thomas was justified in killing the man, wasn't he? After all, this man, together with his friends, killed Ben and his family.*

Farther back, beyond the barn and off to one side, Peter discovered the Berringer family cemetery. It had an iron fence surrounding it and looked somewhat overgrown. The grayish white tombstones held many names of the descendants of the Berringer family. Peter felt a sense of urgency as he rode away from the cemetery. Would he be able to find his brother? In the stillness, as dusk fell, Peter looked heavenward. "I don't have the answers, Lord, but You do. Help me find Thomas soon."

ten

Louisa Bradford hummed a little tune as she carried the mail into the house. She had tried removing Peter from her mind during the past weeks as she involved herself in other interests. Roger Evans was close at hand, and she knew he desired to continue their friendship. It was awkward, her being engaged, and her fiancé out of town. She didn't know where Peter was or when, and if, he planned to return. An evening out with Roger had been enjoyable, and she felt there was nothing wrong with attending a concert with him, especially since he worked for her father and they were just casual friends. Lately she realized her thoughts centered more and more around the charming Mr. Evans. It happened more often than she cared to admit. She chided herself at these times and vowed to discipline her mind and keep her distance.

As she flipped through the pile of mail, she discovered a letter from Peter and her friend, Emily Harris, out in Pennsylvania. Uncertain about which letter to open first, she carried them both into the parlor where her mother sat knitting. "I finally received a letter from Peter after all this time!" she exclaimed handing her mother the rest of the mail. "Now maybe I'll learn some answers to his mysterious disappearance! And another letter from Emily."

Elizabeth Bradford laid her knitted sock in her lap. "Let's hear what Peter has to say, dear. I'm sure he'll clear up this mystery for you. You'll feel so much better knowing where he is."

"All right, I'll read his first. It's not a very lengthy letter. I wonder if he's breaking off our engagement. Perhaps he's found someone else, someone from his past."

"Louisa, you always jump to conclusions. Open Peter's letter, and let's hear what he has to say. The poor boy may be in some kind of trouble."

"Oh, Mother, you are right; perhaps he is in trouble," Louisa said as she tore open the envelope. "I wouldn't want anything to happen to him!" She cleared her throat and read aloud.

> *"My dearest Louisa,*
>   *I am sorry about my hasty departure, but it was imperative I catch the afternoon train to Boston. A problem has arisen in my family, and I prefer not to go into detail at this time. I do not wish to burden you with my problems because I love you too much.*
>   *"Please know that I think of you constantly and keep you in my prayers. I'll try to keep in touch although I'm not sure where I will be. I regret our wedding date must go on hold because I cannot give you any idea of when I will return. Postponing our wedding plans pains me very much. I trust you will understand.*
>   *"I love you, my darling,*
>   *Peter*
> *"P.S. You may write to me at my cousin's address, and she will forward it to me if I have moved on. The address is on the envelope."*

"Well, I don't understand!" Louisa said with a huff as she flung the letter onto her mother's lap. "How dare he speak of love to me!" She stormed across the room and settled in an overstuffed chair, smoothing out her pale blue calico gown and underskirts. "When you truly love someone, you don't keep secrets from them. You share everything! I can't see a life with anyone so mysterious about his wanderings as Peter. I might never know where he is or where he might go from one day to the next! What kind of a life would that be? As far as I'm concerned, it would be no life at all!"

"Really, Louisa, aren't you being a little melodramatic about this?"

"Oh, Mother, you always seem to be on Peter's side about everything. What about me? What about your daughter's feelings? Don't you even care?"

"Of course I do, dear, but you tend to get so carried away. And you're only thinking about yourself. Isn't that rather selfish? What about Peter's feelings? Will you answer his letter as he asked?"

Louisa snorted, jumped up, and grabbed Peter's letter from her mother's lap. "Yes, I'll answer it! I can't wait to write him! And I'll tell him a thing or two while I'm at it. Peter McClough is going to get a newsy letter about a new friend I have, Roger Evans. I'll tell him about a perfect gentleman who doesn't keep a lady waiting or wander around the country on mysterious trips! We'll see how Peter feels about that!" Louisa started toward the stairway with Peter's letter crunched in her hand.

"Wait!" Elizabeth Bradford called. "What about Emily's letter? Aren't you planning to read it to me? I'd like to hear all the news, Louisa."

"I'll read it at the dinner table, Mother, when Father is with us. He'll want to hear the news from Pennsylvania, also. Right now I want to organize my thoughts and get a letter written to Peter. Maybe I'll be a little mysterious, too."

"I think it's best if you cool down some before you write to Peter. You may say something you regret. We can't retrieve unkind words after they are said, or written. Bide your time for a few days. Maybe you'll feel differently by then."

Louisa walked slowly back into the parlor. "I won't feel any differently, Mother. But you're right. I needn't rush like a house on fire. My letter to Peter can wait. I'll be more objective if I give my letter a little more thought."

Elizabeth Bradford glanced through her mail and laid it aside. "Your father will be home early tonight. He seemed a bit nervous about something last evening and didn't sleep well. When I asked him about it this morning, he brushed it aside and said it was nothing. After all these years, I know your father pretty well. I can tell when something is bothering him. I hope it's nothing serious."

"What could it be, Mother?" Louisa asked, a frown knitting her brow. "He isn't ill, is he? He seemed so well and happy when we were in Augusta."

"He was indeed. . .very carefree and lighthearted. It did him good to get away for a week. He and his brother, Phil, have a lot in common. Your father made the trip for your sake, but it was good therapy for him, also. He gets so wound up in his work at the bank."

"But Roger works for him now and takes over much of the responsibility, Mother. I've talked to Roger on several occasions at the bank. He tells me how many contracts he handles in order to make Father's job easier. He's glad to be so helpful and doesn't know how Father got along without him."

Elizabeth Bradford's face broke into a smile at her daughter's enthusiastic words. "That sounds like Roger, all right. I'm sure he feels he is the best thing that happened to the First Bank of Waterville. . .or even the whole of Waterville for that matter."

"Well, it's true, Mother," Louisa insisted. "I'm sure Father appreciates all his time and input. Roger deserves a promotion and larger salary."

"Did he mention that to you by any chance?"

"Well, he did. . .sort of. . .very casually one afternoon at the bank. He can't get by on the salary he makes now. He'd like to buy a home and make plans for the future."

"Roger hasn't been with the bank long enough to warrant a promotion, Louisa."

"How long does it take? If someone is as industrious as Roger, they should be able to move up in the company."

"Your father worked for his father for many years before

he took over the bank. Your grandpa handed him the top job when he decided to step down and take life a little easier. Your father will do the same some day."

"Who will that be, Mother? Roger, maybe?"

"Since we didn't have a son, your father doesn't have an heir to carry on at the bank. He will groom someone for the position. And yes, it may be Roger Evans. Or whomever you marry, Louisa. Your husband may be the one to carry on the Bradford tradition. His name will be different, but he will be family."

Louisa's lips curved into a big smile. "Roger Evans—president of the Bradford family bank someday. Won't that be grand?"

The front door slammed as Jack Bradford entered the parlor from the hallway. "What's so grand, Louisa?" he asked as he pulled off his overcoat, hat, and gloves. "It's certainly not the weather. There's a misty rain in the air."

Louisa gave her father a hug and took his coat from him. "It's grand that you are home, Father," she smiled impishly rubbing her hands across his knitted brow. "I have a letter from Emily Harris in Pennsylvania. I've waited to read it to you and Mother at the dinner table."

"And a nice letter from Peter, also," Elizabeth Bradford added.

"Good!" he replied and bent to kiss Elizabeth. "I'll wash up and join you in the dining room shortly."

Louisa shared Peter's letter with her father during the meal but saved Emily's letter until they finished the main course. "Emily is my sweet friend," Louisa announced, "so I'll read her letter while we eat dessert. I've told her all about my friend, Roger Evans, and I'm anxious to read her reply." Louisa opened the pale pink envelope and smoothed the letter with her fingers.

"Dear Louisa,
    It is always exciting to get your letters and hear all

the news from back home. I'm very surprised about your friendship with Roger Evans, especially since you and Peter are engaged. From what you say, Roger sounds very nice, handsome, thoughtful, and a real gentleman. But you and Peter are the perfect couple, so I'm thankful your relationship with Roger is strictly platonic. We know Peter loves you very much. His sudden departure with no explanation has us all confused. We can't imagine what problem drove him away. Letters from my folks, Cassie and Bill, and Fred and Sarah have added no light to the problem. Peter did not confide in them, left abruptly, and sent no word as to his whereabouts. He loves Ma's cooking and often stopped by whenever he could. And Peter and Fred are such close friends. It seems he would have shared his problem with Fred even if he couldn't share it with you. Well, whatever it is, some day the story will come out.

"The new church building is coming along well, and we hope to be in by Christmas. Robert and the men work long hours, every spare minute they can. I'm working on a children's Christmas program, and the youngsters are enthusiastic about it. I've coaxed Jim Bishop's two children into having parts, and they are coming out of their shells. The interaction with other children is good for them. Mrs. Bishop offered to help in any way she could. She is still very shy, but I can include her in small ways. I think it is good for her to feel needed. She seems happier when she works with the children. We're praying the program will have an impact on Mr. Bishop if he will attend. Jim Bishop is extremely bullheaded, and Robert grieves about his backbiting. Jim's antagonistic ways tend to stir up discord among the brethren. Finally, Robert and his deacons visited Jim at his home and approached the subject. They reprimanded him, in a kind and Christian manner, regarding his accusations.

Jim was insulted. He threatened and did pull his membership out of the church. This seems to be best for everyone concerned. Thankfully he has allowed his wife and children to continue to attend and be involved. Please pray for Jim Bishop. He professes to be a Christian, but his actions surely must grieve the Lord.

"Our ladies' guild meets once a month to sew baby layettes and make quilts. Samuel's wife, Ellie, comes and also my aunt Sophie. We bring our lunch and have a good time of fellowship and prayer in one of the larger farm homes. About ten ladies and several little children who are not yet school age attend. I know I haven't been married long, but I am eager to have a baby. All my family write to me about my niece, Rebeccah, and nephew, Freddy. They tell me all the sweet things the little ones are doing. Some day I hope to have a precious little child of my own.

"Let me know any news you hear about Peter. He is very dear to our family. You asked about Christmas. We won't get home for the holidays this year. I'll miss seeing you, my family, and the old homestead. Waterville is so beautiful at this time of year, but it is our first Christmas since our marriage. It will be special to be together as husband and wife here in Pennsylvania. The lovely, rolling hills and valleys remind me of my family home in Maine. It is beautiful country, and you must visit us whenever you can.

"Love, your friend always,
Emily"

eleven

Peter mounted Thunder and headed away from the plantation toward the iron gates at the roadway. The warm and muggy night air closed in upon him as dusk fused into darkness. A moon sliver offered little light, and he strained his eyes in the vespertine inkiness around him. As Peter turned Thunder toward town, he heard hoofbeats coming from behind. He gave Thunder his head and urged him into a gallop. The hoofbeats following them grew closer as Peter bent low over his charge and allowed the animal to do what he did best—ride like the wind. When a shot rang out in the night, Peter felt a chill run up and down his spine.

"Someone wants to kill me," he muttered. "Why? I've done nothing!" Another shot rang out loud and clear, but Peter realized it was high above his head. Thunder shook his head, whinnied, and picked up his already rapid pace. "Steady, fella," Peter whispered as they raced faster, and the other hoofbeats grew dimmer. "I reckon whoever it is just wants to scare us. I get the feeling they don't like Yankees in the South."

When Peter realized the renegade was no longer tailing him, he pulled Thunder to a slow trot. "No use getting all sweaty in this heat, fella. We both need to do a little cooling off." Peter eased into town and located a stable about a block off the main street. After rubbing down his magnificent animal, he paid the stable master for Thunder's feed and overnight lodging. Thunder nuzzled his master, and Peter stroked the fine animal before heading toward town. He found the small cafe he had seen earlier in the day and ordered a hearty meal. The place was nearly deserted due to the lateness of the hour. A few people eyed him suspiciously and whispered among themselves, but no one gave him any trouble, and he left the cafe fully satisfied by the tasty meal. The inn on the opposite corner was clean and comfortable, and he purchased a room for one night. It was a relief to get out of his dusty clothes, wash up, and stretch out on the bed.

"What do I do next?" he murmured lazily. "Thomas isn't at the plantation, and people here don't want me to ask questions about him or the Berringer place." Peter yawned and felt himself drifting off to sleep. The trip had taken its toll on the young man. "Being tailed tonight from the Berringer place was. . . ," a yawn broke into his musings, "exciting. Tomorrow I'll think about what to do next—tomorrow when my head is a little clearer."

Peter finished his breakfast at the cafe the following morning and lingered over his second cup of strong coffee. As he eyed the other patrons, he concluded the Southern folk were not that much different from the Northerners. *We are all created in God's image with a free will to choose God and His Son. We live, we work, we dream, we fall in love. We have families that we care about. It's too bad the Civil War had to happen and cause some to have bad feelings toward others. God tells us in the Bible to love one another.*

An attractive young lady and an older woman entered the cafe at that moment. Peter realized it was the same young woman he spoke to in town the day before. Quickly he stood up and caught their attention. "Pardon me, Miss. We met yesterday when I asked for some directions. Won't you and your companion join me at my table?"

Genevieve Markam whirled around and faced Peter. Her violet eyes opened wide at his suggestion. A slight gasp echoed from the curved lips. "You are a stranger, Sir, and we do not care to share a table with you. Come, Mother!" She reached for the older woman's arm and pulled her toward the far side of the room.

"Who is that young man, Genevieve?" Mrs. Markam demanded loudly. "I've never seen him before. He's obviously a Yankee by his speech. Where did you meet him?"

Peter watched as the cafe patrons turned in their seats and eyed the ladies as they settled into chairs at a small table in the rear.

"Where did you meet him, Genevieve?" Mrs. Markam demanded again, more loudly than before. Peter rose and moved toward their table.

"I didn't meet him, Mother," Genevieve said softly in an attempt to soothe her mother. She patted her chestnut tresses peeking from beneath her bonnet. "He's a Northerner, and I saw him in town yesterday. He asked me for directions. That's all. I don't even know his name."

"I can remedy that," Peter smiled as he reached their table, his mug of coffee in one hand. "May I sit down?"

"No!" Genevieve shouted. "Leave us alone!"

"Genevieve, that is no way to treat a stranger in town," Mrs. Markam insisted. "Where is your Southern hospitality? Forgive my daughter's rudeness, Sir. Perhaps I can help you with directions. I've lived in this area much longer than my daughter."

"Thank you, but I received directions from the ticket master yesterday. My name is Peter McClough and I'm from Waterville, Maine."

"My, you are a long way off, young man. I'm Harriet Markam, and this is my daughter Genevieve. Won't you join us?"

"Thank you, Mrs. Markam," Peter said as he took a seat beside Genevieve. "I'm just finishing my second cup of coffee before I leave. May I ask you for some information regarding the Berringer Plantation?"

Mrs. Markam gasped and caught at her throat. Her face paled as she slumped in her seat. Genevieve jumped up from her chair and put her arm around her mother. She patted her face and pushed back stray strands of gray hair. "Mother!" she cried. "Are you all right?"

Peter, brow furrowed, fanned Mrs. Markam with his hat and patted her hand. Genevieve pushed him away and cried, "Now, look what you've done!"

"I'm so sorry," Peter cried. "Did I say something wrong?"

Mrs. Markam moaned, sat upright, and glared at Peter. "Young man," she said slowly, "why are you interested in the Berringer Plantation? And what business is it of yours. . .a Northerner?"

Peter pushed back a shock of dark hair and let his fingers run through it. Should he tell these people his business? How else could he find out more about Thomas? Would it be hurtful to Thomas to confess that he was his brother? He hesitated, at a loss for words. Finally, with a prayer in his heart, he spoke slowly and softly. "I realize you are disturbed by my mention of the Berringer Plantation, Mrs. Markam, just as Genevieve was yesterday. I am sorry. Thomas Hayes, the foster son of the Berringers' is my half brother. I came south to see if I could find him. We have never met. I only learned a short time ago that I had a brother. We fought on different sides during the war, but thankfully I did not know it."

Mrs. Markam looked at Peter through teary eyes. "Did you know, Mr. McClough, your brother killed a man at his plantation?"

Peter lowered his eyes. "I heard about it through a distant cousin of mine, Mrs. Markam. It was very sad news. But do you know the reason, the circumstances under which he committed this crime?"

"There is never a justifiable reason to kill someone, Mr. McClough," Mrs. Markham said dabbing at her eyes with her handkerchief.

"Do you know my brother well?" Peter asked. "If so, you would be a better judge of his character than I."

Genevieve Markam held out her left hand and displayed a

diamond on the third finger. "I know Thomas better than anyone else," she said with difficulty, "We are engaged to be married."

Peter's face constricted in pain. "This must be very hard for you, Genevieve. I wish I could make it easier. My cousin Annabelle, who lives near Boston, raised Thomas until he was ten years old. At that time he became a ward of the Berringer family. Annabelle and I are very concerned about him. I would give anything to find my brother and get his crime resolved."

"It's impossible!" Mrs. Markam cried. "He has to pay for his crime."

"Mother, don't excite yourself. You know what the doctor said."

"I know! I know! My heart could give out at any time. Well, I won't be satisfied until I see that young man pay with his life. He needs to hang for his crime."

"But why, Mrs. Markam? Why are you so bitter?" Peter asked. "The man my brother killed was one of a group of men who killed four persons, for no reason, on the Berringer Plantation. They were Thomas's dear friends. Thomas reacted hastily out of anger, which was wrong. But I must find him as soon as possible. Due to the circumstances surrounding the crime, the law might be lenient if he turns himself in."

"He already did, Mr. McClough. Thomas came back to Nashville a few weeks ago and turned himself in. They are deliberating now what punishment he must endure," Genevieve said sadly. "We have a new sheriff since the incident happened. Perhaps you can talk to him on your brother's behalf."

"What are you saying, Genevieve?" Mrs. Markam cried, her face aghast. "Do you want Thomas to be acquitted of his crime? How could you?"

"I love him, Mother, and always will."

"Rubbish! Take that ring off your finger at once! My daughter will not marry a criminal!"

"I know it's a serious crime, Mrs. Markam, but God teaches us from the Bible about forgiveness. Jesus forgave all sinners—thieves, murderers, and tax collectors. Can't we do the same? The man Thomas killed was himself a murderer. He killed four of Thomas's friends. Put yourself in his place. Can't you forgive him for his crime?"

"Never!" Mrs. Markam ranted as the cafe patrons looked on. "I will never forgive him! Thomas Hayes killed Clay Prescott, my only brother, in cold blood!"

Peter sat spellbound, his mouth gaped, as one in shock. He let out a deep sigh and asked softly, "The man Thomas killed was your brother, Genevieve's uncle?"

Mrs. Markam cried softly into her handkerchief. "My only brother! He's been an anchor to me since my husband's death four years ago. Dear Clay was the only stability we had in our lives." Mrs. Markam blew her nose and struggled to continue. "Genevieve and I are completely alone in this world now. My son, Adam, died of battle wounds early in the war. It broke my husband's heart. He grieved for Adam until his death of consumption."

"I can't tell you how sorry I am," Peter said sincerely. "Is there anything I can do for you?"

"We'll manage, Mr. McClough," Genevieve said, "but thank you for your offer of help. Mother worries about losing our home. Our slaves left long ago, right after the war. My uncle Clay hired men to plant the fields, and Mother and I managed fine under his care. He had no family, so he moved into our home and took over where Father left off. We had no idea Uncle was a member of a secret terrorist organization. It gives me chills to think about the destruction and chaos this society causes. Mother and I need to beg Thomas's pardon for Uncle Clay's part in the deaths of his friends. We want no part of this organization."

"It is hard to understand the reasoning behind such a movement," Peter said. "And I'm certain most Southerners are not agreeable to their practices."

"If it is any comfort," Genevieve offered, "we found a handwritten note of my uncle's after his death. It must have been written right before the attack at the Berringer Plantation. His exact words were, 'I am sick of this organization and its evil destruction. I will tell the men tonight that I want out. This will be my last escapade. Forgive me, God, for all the killing and havoc we have caused.' Finding this note was a great comfort to Mother and me. We believe my uncle misjudged the organization when he became involved. When he finally realized it before his death, he desired to leave the Klan."

"His note must be a great comfort to you both. I wish your uncle had retired before the escapade at the Berringer place, but we can't change the situation. I must talk to the sheriff about Thomas's crime. Perhaps he will listen. Good-bye, ladies. I'm sorry we met under such sad circumstances." Peter drank the balance of his coffee which was already cold, stood to his feet, grabbed his hat, and left the cafe.

He went by the stable and paid for another day's lodging for his horse. His feet dragged as he headed toward the jailhouse located a few blocks away. Could he attempt to justify Thomas's crime? And how would Thomas react to a brother he had never seen? Was it a mistake for him, a Yankee, to come to this place and try to get his brother exonerated? The sheriff might throw him out—or worse yet, put him in jail. These thoughts permeated his mind until beads of sweat stood out on his forehead. He was unused to Tennessee's warm, muggy fall weather. As he hesitated before the jailhouse, Peter pulled his bandana from his pocket and wiped the moisture from his brow and face.

Mustering all his courage, he pulled on the heavy wooden door of the jailhouse and entered a small room. A medium built man about forty years old sat at a desk just inside the door. He looked up as the door creaked to a close. "What can

I do for you, stranger?" he asked, cheerfully. "Are you new in town?"

"Yes, Sir. I arrived yesterday," Peter replied, knowing his Yankee dialect would give him away. "I would like to have a word with you."

The sheriff folded the paper he had been reading, shoved back his chair, extended his hand, and smiled broadly. "Have our citizens been bothering you or are you in some kind of trouble? I'll be glad to help in whatever way I can. Pull up a chair and sit down."

Peter grabbed a wooden chair from the corner and moved it closer to the sheriff's desk. "I have an unusual request, Sheriff. I understand Thomas Hayes is confined here because he killed a man on his estate, the Berringer Plantation."

"That's right," the sheriff drawled. "Is he wanted for a crime somewhere else? Is that why you came?"

"Nothing like that," Peter said quickly. "I am Peter McClough, Thomas Hayes' half brother, from Waterville, Maine. I have an older cousin in Boston who informed me of the circumstances of the crime. It appears to us Thomas had every right to fire at the terrorist society band for killing his friend and his friend's family."

The sheriff eyed Peter keenly. "It is a sad situation, Mr. McClough. What happened at the Berringer Plantation was a terrible atrocity. I have only been sheriff a little over a week. Your brother was already incarcerated when I replaced the former sheriff. Since my arrival, I have cracked down on this secret society. Notices have gone out over the county that I will not tolerate any terrorist actions. Any caught involved in such action will be punished severely."

"That's good to hear, Sheriff," Peter said. "But what about my brother? Must he pay for his crime under the unusual circumstances?"

"The killing of another human being is wrong, Mr. McClough, regardless of the situation. No one should take the law into his own hands. Justice must prevail."

"But, Sheriff," Peter blurted, "what will you do to him? Will my brother hang for his crime?"

The sheriff eyed the distraught young man before him. "No decision has been settled as yet, Mr. McClough. We are thoroughly investigating the death of the man killed. His niece brought in a note he wrote the night he died. . .before leaving for the Berringer Plantation. It is evident he planned to leave the Klan that very night and informed them of his decision. I have some recent information that may put light on the subject, but I am not at liberty to discuss it."

Peter frowned. "It doesn't look good for my brother, does it Sheriff? Could. . .could I see him for a few minutes? We've never met, and I think it's about time we do."

The sheriff pushed back his chair and stood up. "Of course you can see him. Take as long as you like. A visit from his brother will cheer Thomas up. We've had some fine chats, he and I. I like your brother, Mr. McClough. I like him a lot!"

Peter's face relaxed into a slight grin. "Thanks, Sheriff. And call me Peter, won't you? It seems friendlier, somehow."

Peter followed the sheriff down a short passageway to a set of cells. Behind the first one sat a young man, head in his hands. He looked up as the sheriff and Peter approached and Peter noticed the shock of dark hair, so like his own. Dark, sad eyes stared blankly from the man's unshaven face. The man blinked his eyes several times and pushed his dark hair back from his forehead. His eyes seemed sunken in the pale face, which registered despair. "Someone to see me, Sheriff?" he asked. "I hope it's not a lot of questions again about the shooting. That night stands out so vivid in my mind. I dread recalling it one more time."

"No, Thomas, no questions this time. You have a special visitor. He's come a long way to see you."

"Hello Thomas," Peter said with emotion. "I'm your brother, Peter McClough. Annabelle told me all about you."

Thomas rushed over to the bars and stuck his hand through, which Peter clasped in his own. "And Annabelle told me all about you, Peter. I left Annabelle's place several weeks ago because I didn't want to get either of you involved. But I'm glad you came. Thanks, brother." His eyes gathered moisture as he spoke.

The sheriff pulled out a key and opened the cell door. "Come out and visit with your brother for a while, Thomas. We'll put a couple chairs in the hallway so you'll be more comfortable. You two must have a lot to talk about."

"Aren't you afraid I'll make a break for it, Sheriff?" Thomas asked, his lips curled in a smile.

"My instincts tell me you won't try anything, Thomas. From all the talks we've had together, I think I know you fairly well. After all, you did return a few weeks ago on your own and turn yourself in."

"Maybe my brother came down here to help me escape. Did you consider that possibility? The two of us could overpower you easily," Thomas joked.

"Sure you could. But I don't think you will. I'm a pretty good judge of character. Now you fellows enjoy your visit together while I go back to my paperwork." The sheriff grinned. "And let me know when you want back into your cell."

Peter looked long and hard at his brother. Although their coloring was the same, Thomas was taller and a little thinner. There was no mistake about the resemblance, especially through the dark eyes and shock of unruly hair. They stared at each other for several moments without saying a word. Then Peter, his eyes moist with tears, threw his arms around Thomas's shoulders. The pair stood quietly for a time, too moved to speak.

An hour later they had covered every detail of one another's lives. Each had heard much of it from Annabelle but savored the stories firsthand. Peter assured his brother he would stay in

Nashville until the situation was resolved. "I'll get the best lawyer I can find and get you out of here somehow!"

"Move out of the inn this afternoon and into my place," Thomas insisted. "The sheriff has the key to my plantation in the front office. Pick up your horse from the stable and mine also. I left my bay mare at the stable several weeks ago when I turned myself in. She's a beauty with white patches on her face. I call her Powder. The sheriff keeps tabs on her for me. He says she's still there—doing okay. The stable bill might be high, but I'll pay you back when and if I get out of here. If they hang me. . ." His voice drifted off and he swallowed hard. "Anyway, if something happens to me, sell the plantation and all the furniture. I want you, Genevieve, and Annabelle to share the money."

Thomas talked about Genevieve, his betrothed, and about his great love for her. "Even if I could get out of this situation, it's all over for us, Peter. I killed her uncle, and she'll never forgive me."

"Don't be so sure of that," Peter said, as he explained his earlier meeting with Genevieve and her mother at the cafe. "She is a lovely young woman, Thomas. And she declared emphatically, in the presence of her mother, that she still loves you."

Thomas jumped up and walked back and forth, his hands folded as if in prayer. "Could it be possible? Dare I hope that it is so?"

Just then they heard the jailhouse door open and a feminine voice speak. "Hello Sheriff. I've come to see Thomas. I know his brother is here, but could I speak with him a few moments?" It was Genevieve's voice, and Thomas looked dazed. He started toward the office with Peter close behind him. They heard the sheriff speak.

"Of course, Miss Markam. I'm certain he would like to see you. Thomas speaks of you often. I understand the two of you are engaged to be married."

"Yes," she said softly. "I hope we can still carry out our plans."

Thomas rounded the corner at that moment and rushed toward his sweetheart. "Genny! I didn't think you would come after what happened to your uncle. I've longed to see you. . .to hear your voice."

Genevieve Markam walked boldly into Thomas's arms and he pulled her close. His head bent over the chestnut curls as they rested against his shoulder.

"I didn't think there was any hope for us," he murmured huskily. "I'm sorry about your uncle." Then recovering his composure, he introduced Genevieve to Peter. "But you already met my brother," he laughed. "Isn't it wonderful? Peter came all the way down to Tennessee to help me out of this mess. He thinks I should be exonerated because of the circumstances, but. . . , " his voice trailed off to a whisper, "I am still guilty, Genny. I was so upset about Ben's death, I shot and killed a man, a man who turned out to be your Uncle Clay."

Genny put her fingers against Thomas's lips as if to quiet him. "Don't speak of it, Thomas. It was a tragic thing. My mother and I regret what also happened to Ben and his family. We never knew my uncle was involved in such a terroristic society. He planned to leave the Klan after that last evening. We found a note saying he was sick of their activities and wanted out. I gave the note to the sheriff a few days ago. He thinks it might have some bearing on the case."

"I didn't tell you, Thomas, because I didn't want to get your hopes up," the sheriff said. "Any information I can gather may help. But it's time to take you back to your cell. If the wrong person came in and found you in the front office, he'd be on my neck. Peter and Miss Markam can visit you in the back."

"I can't stay," Genevieve said. "Mother is so upset about this situation. I left her at home for a few minutes. She thinks I'm posting a letter and mustn't know about this visit. I need to get back to her. She's edgy these days and needs extra care."

The pair embraced, and Thomas kissed her lightly on the cheek. "Good-bye, my darling," he whispered. "I can face anything as long as I know you are on my side. Pray for me."

"Of course, dear Thomas," she whispered breathlessly as Peter and the sheriff turned away and tried not to listen. "I pray for you every day. I will visit you again tomorrow and the next day and the next. Until they let you out of this terrible place!" Turning to go, she asked, "Is there any hope, Sheriff? Dare I hope that someday Thomas will be free?"

"There is always hope, Miss Markam. I am investigating this case thoroughly. As I told Peter McClough earlier, I may have some further information soon, something I cannot disclose at present. Yes, Miss Markam, I assure you, there is always hope!"

twelve

"Fantastic!" Louisa exclaimed, as she waved her letter and whirled around the Bradford parlor. "Clara and Sam Burns are getting married over Thanksgiving weekend, Mother. She wants me to stand up with her. Our family is invited for Thanksgiving dinner, and the wedding is on the following Saturday afternoon. Of course we'll go, won't we?"

Elizabeth Bradford laid her handwork carefully on the cushion beside her. "I'm sure your father will want to go, dear. This is an important occasion. He will want to see his only niece getting married. I'll make a note of the date so we can plan on it."

Later, when Jack Bradford returned from his bank, Louisa greeted him and shared the news. "We must go, Father. Clara and her parents are our only living relatives. This is an important wedding for the Bradford families."

Elizabeth Bradford entered from the dining room. "Louisa is excited about the wedding, dear," she said giving her husband a peck on the cheek. "I must confess I am, also. I'm sure we are all thankful Clara gave up grieving over her lost love and re-entered the real world. Sam Burns is a fine young man."

"Oh yes, Father," Louisa said. "Sam is quite the catch, really. I found him a genuine and kind person. Clara and Sam will be very happy together."

Jack Bradford cleared his throat. "Ahem! Yes, yes, I agree. But most important of all, Sam is a fine, dedicated Christian. I talked with him after church at some length, and he appeared to have a heart for the Lord. That's more than I can say for Roger Evans. You talk to him a lot at the bank, Louisa. Why haven't we seen him in church lately?"

"Roger is busy, Father. He does so much extra work for you at the bank. I'm afraid you pile many extra duties on him that keep him after hours. Sundays he needs his rest. He reminds me how hard he works to keep the bank in good running order."

"Rubbish!" Jack Bradford exclaimed. "He has the same hours the rest of the employees do. I admit he's a hard worker. He spends a lot of time in the back room and goes over the files constantly, but it's his choice. I've reminded him it isn't necessary. I'll have an auditor come in before the Christmas holiday."

"Is anything wrong, Jack?" Elizabeth asked. "I thought the auditor didn't come until spring."

"No. . .no. . .of course not. Nothing is wrong. I merely decided to have an audit made earlier this time. I want to make sure all the accounts are in order before the first of the year."

"Well, dear, I have one of your favorite meals tonight. A beef roast with potatoes, onions, and carrots. And homemade bread."

"And fresh apple pie, Mother," Louisa added. "Don't forget Father's favorite pie."

Jack Bradford chuckled as he surveyed his wife and daughter. "It sounds like a feast fit for a king. I'm a little suspicious of my two girls, though. Is this special dinner a bribe to make sure I'll take you to Clara's wedding in Augusta? If so, you needn't have bothered. I wouldn't miss the wedding of my brother's only child. We Bradfords must stick together!"

᷍

When Louisa visited her father's bank later that week, Roger Evans asked her to attend another dinner and concert for a little outing together—as friends. Louisa, pleased at his offer, accepted—her face aglow with color. Her social life had been curtailed with Peter away, and she missed concerts and dinners out. Surely, she reasoned, it wouldn't be wrong to attend a casual dinner and concert with one of her father's employees. Their friendship had grown and blossomed through her many visits to the bank, and she accepted his invitation graciously. Although her parents seemed to disapprove, Louisa looked forward to the outing. She had received another letter from Peter which said he was in Tennessee. He still did not disclose any information about his mysterious trip. Upset and frustrated, Louisa penned a hasty letter, in care of his cousin, Annabelle Hayes.

> *"Dear Peter,*
>
> *"I'm sorry to be so long in writing to you. I don't understand why you cannot confide in me about the mystery of your trip, especially since we are engaged. I thought when two people were in love, they would share everything with one another. I must tell you that I refuse to endure such secrecy.*
>
> *"I also need to be honest with you and inform you I am seeing someone else. It is only a friendship, for now. His name is Roger Evans, and he works for my father at his bank. He is a fine young man who seems to care a great deal about me. It is nice to have someone take me to dinner and concerts. I don't know what the future holds, since I am seeing more and more of Roger Evans. Frankly, Peter, your brief letters are not enough.*
>
> > *"Sincerely,*
> > *Louisa"*

On the way to the restaurant, Louisa told Roger about her cousin Clara's upcoming wedding and how delighted her family was. She explained that she would stand up for Clara as her maid of honor.

"How nice," Roger said as the horses clip-clopped along the roadway. "And when will this wedding take place?"

"The Saturday after Thanksgiving. We'll leave by train on

Wednesday and be there for Thanksgiving. Then we'll travel home on Sunday after church, so Father won't miss too many days at the bank."

Roger laughed. "Your father needn't be concerned about his bank. I'll be here, and I'll take charge! Jack Bradford can count on me to keep everything under control."

"I know you will, Roger. Father depends on you because you are devoted to your job. He mentioned how much time you spend reviewing the files." Louisa sighed. "I don't know what Father would do without you. But don't worry. Your workload will be easier after Christmas."

"Why is that?" Roger demanded as he reined in the team and brought the horses to a halt. They had arrived at the restaurant, and Roger climbed down to secure the team to the hitching post. Lanterns lit a pathway and illuminated the cozy eating establishment. As he reached to lift Louisa down, he asked once again. "Why will my workload be easier? Does your father plan to hire another assistant?"

"Mercy, no!" Louisa exclaimed. "He mentioned bringing the auditor in early because he wants to make sure all accounts are in order by the first of the year."

"But. . .but Louisa," Roger faltered. His usually handsome face knit into a frown and looked agitated. "Why is your father changing the time schedule all of a sudden? I thought the auditor didn't come until spring."

Louisa's merry little laugh rang out clear as a bell. "Mother asked the same thing. Isn't that strange? But Father decided to have it done in December this year."

Roger, his lips pursed tightly together, steered Louisa almost roughly into the restaurant, and the waitress settled them at a small table near the back. He plunked himself down in his chair and stared at Louisa long and hard. "I don't like it, Louisa! I don't like it at all."

"What don't you like, Roger? The atmosphere here is lovely."

"No!" Roger snapped, rather loudly. Louisa, startled, looked at him wide-eyed, embarrassed as people near them turned in their seats. Roger lowered his voice and whispered harshly, "I mean about the auditor coming early. There is no reason for it. No reason at all."

Louisa reached over and patted his hand. "Don't fret about it, Roger. It isn't important. It has nothing to do with you."

"Of course not!" Roger's face relaxed in a slight smile and his lips curled over his teeth. "It doesn't mean a thing."

Roger, quieter than usual, chewed his food thoughtfully. Louisa enjoyed each morsel and oohed and aahed over the tempting dessert. She tried to keep the atmosphere light and gay. It was unusual to see Roger in such a serious mood, so she shared humorous bits of news gleaned from letters sent by her friend, Emily, in Pennsylvania. Roger's occasional halfhearted response displayed a lack of attention. She could not understand his mood change but decided he suffered from overwork. His mood at the concert remained the same, and the ride home seemed dreary and uninteresting. Roger sat rigid, deep in thought. Usually a good conversationalist, who kept her laughing until her sides ached, he was no longer a fun-loving companion. His tales of past escapades and jokes seemed forgotten. Louisa glanced sideways at his set mouth and knitted brow. What had happened to change his temperament?

Louisa sighed audibly. "Bother! I don't know what's troubling you, Roger, but you are out of sorts about something. Did I do or say the wrong thing this evening? If so, tell me and perhaps I can correct it."

"No! No! It's nothing you did or said! I'm fine, just fine. My mind is on other things, that's all. Nothing of interest to you."

"I'm going to tell Father you are simply overworked and can't even enjoy an evening out with me. He mustn't heap bunches of accounts on you anymore. After all, you are only human. One man can do only so much!"

Roger feigned a little smile. "Don't worry your pretty little head about my problems, Louisa. And don't nag your father about overworking me. I only do what I have to do. Let's forget this conversation, shall we? Now then, shall we take a ride along the river tonight?" Roger pulled a blanket from under the seat and handed it to Louisa. "Wrap yourself in this. It will keep you toasty-warm in the night air."

A little shiver escaped Louisa's lips as she took the gray blanket and wrapped it around her shoulders. She was glad she had worn a heavy wool skirt and warm boots. Her legs and feet were warm enough, but the chill reached deep into her back and shoulders. "This feels much better, Roger. There's a full moon, and I love to see the moonbeams dance on the river. We'll have snow before long, and it won't be as pleasant as it is tonight."

The ride by the river left Louisa breathless. A bright moon cast deep shadows from the buildings across the way. Fishing boats tied to the wharf bobbed up and down in the soft breeze. Some couples, bundled warmly, walked arm in arm along the riverfront or sat on benches. Louisa shivered from the cold, and Roger reached over and put an arm around her shoulders, drawing her to him. Louisa felt the warmth of his body next to hers and leaned against his shoulder. She felt warm and serene.

"Let's elope, Louisa!" Roger said impulsively. "I'll take you home so you can pack a bag. We'll leave tonight and go wherever you want. Just name the place!"

Louisa gasped and pushed Roger away. "What are you saying? We're only good friends, remember? I'm still engaged to Peter McClough! Where did you come up with such a ridiculous idea? And anyway, I want to have a church wedding. . .with family and friends in attendance."

"Peter's gone. Who knows where he is or when he will return, and you're beginning not to care anymore. Admit it Louisa! You don't care if Peter comes back. And you care for me a whole lot more than you let on. I can see it in your eyes. All the time you've spent at the bank lately. . .just talking to me, laughing with me. You gave me hope. I thought sure, in time you would break your engagement. Why did you encourage me?"

Louisa looked down at her gloved hands and wrung them together. A frown knitted her brow. "I. . .I do like you, Roger, very much, and I enjoy being with you. It was wrong of me to encourage you, especially since I'm wearing Peter's ring. I've told him about you, about our friendship in a letter, and I may break off the engagement in the near future. He's not being fair to me."

"Peter's gone, Louisa! I'm here!" Roger said brashly. "I want to elope with you tonight!"

"Take me home, Roger, right *now!*" Louisa drew the blanket closer around her shoulders. "I don't want to hear any more of this nonsense about eloping. It's out of the question!"

Roger Evans scowled. "I guess you are just a child, after all! If you were a real woman, you would forget Peter and elope with me tonight! Well," he said as he snapped the reins over the team's flanks, "perhaps it is better this way!"

The ride to the Bradford home seemed longer than usual. Louisa noticed Roger's irate spirit and tried to carry on a conversation. He looked straight ahead and rejected her every effort to lighten the atmosphere. Grim-faced and brow furrowed, Roger sat in silence during the ride to her home. He brought the team to a halt in front of the large brownstone, glanced at Louisa, and nodded. He made no effort to help her down from the carriage. She removed the blanket from around her shoulders, folded it neatly, and climbed down by herself.

"Thank you for the lovely dinner and concert, Roger," she said softly. "I hope you feel better in the morning." He nodded his head, grunted some unintelligible words, and pulled away in a fury.

thirteen

Peter McClough whistled a familiar tune as he brushed down Powder and Thunder. The horses seemed to enjoy one another's company and the freedom to roam the large pastures during the day. He had cleaned their stalls and loaded in hay and water for the animals. It was several weeks since he settled into the Berringer Plantation, his brother Thomas's home. Peter felt almost lost in the huge estate. His own home in Waterville was large and somewhat elegant, but it did not compare with this. Thomas's beautiful antebellum home, nestled in a grove of trees, boasted a wide veranda across the front. Floors, covered with wide plank pine wood and expensive carpets met his eyes while fine paintings and tapestries graced the walls. A brilliant mahogany spiral staircase led to the upstairs, which featured a number of bedrooms and dressing rooms. All were expensively furnished with luscious fabrics surrounding the tall four-postered and canopied beds. Peter spent time studying the family portraits lining the walls and the staircase. This estate would accommodate a wealthy Southern family with servants in the finest style.

After completing his tour of the house, Peter finally settled his belongings in the smallest upstairs bedroom available. It had a single canopy bed, dresser, commode, and washstand on the far wall. Pale yellow curtains dressed the windows and canopy enclosure with matching pillows and coverlet on the bed. Peter appreciated the coziness of the smaller room and the family pictures which lined one wall. When he studied them, he found some contained pictures of Thomas at various ages of his life. Sometimes he lit the small fireplace on the far wall to ward off the chill. The days were still warm in Tennessee, but some nights became nippy as the temperatures dropped. And Peter enjoyed laying the logs, plenty of which were available on the property. Then he would sit in the old wicker rocker and gaze deeply into the crackling fire—his mind filled with thoughts of his dear Louisa. During these times he crowded out the despair of having a brother in jail, one he had just come to know, one who might be hung on the gallows for murder.

He had hired a lawyer for the case who seemed understanding and trustworthy, but as yet the lawyer had turned up no new evidence. Each day Peter rode into town, consulted with the lawyer, and visited his brother for several hours. He alternated riding Powder and Thunder in order to give each of the animals some exercise. Peter never mentioned the incident of his first evening to Thomas about the renegade who fired at him when he left the plantation. There seemed to be no reason to do so as there had been no mishap since.

Peter had written letters to Annabelle and Louisa and posted them earlier. He tried to give Annabelle hope, although he had no concrete evidence as to how the case would be settled. He assured her a lawyer handled the case, and Thomas was well and safe in the county jail. In closing he said, "Thomas sends his love, Annabelle, and so do I."

&

Louisa wondered about Roger's change of character. She tried mentally to sort out her feelings for the man. She had to admit an attraction for Roger, but his moody character the other evening upset her. How could he be kind and attentive one moment and angry the next? If he cared about her in a proper way, wouldn't her desires matter to him? He had boldly suggested they elope, so he must care for her a great deal. But he only seemed concerned with himself, what he wanted, and not her desires. Her parents had warned her about his lack of interest in spiritual things, but she refused to listen. She had been caught up in his attentiveness at a time when she felt neglected and unloved by Peter. She realized Roger had fulfilled the selfish desires of her own heart by showering attention on her. The dinners and concerts filled a void and restored her spirit.

And what about Peter? His letters confirmed he loved her and missed her, but she felt letters were not enough to prove his love. What a foolish goose she had been! She had written him a letter and told him about Roger Evans. The letter intimated that Roger cared for her, and of course, Peter would assume the feeling was mutual. What had she said exactly, and what would Peter think of her now? Would he think she was fickle and childish? She supposed she was, to a point. Could he forgive her foolishness and still love her? And was Peter the one she wanted—or Roger? These thoughts filled her mind constantly.

Louisa's skirts swished about her as she entered the parlor where her mother worked on her daughter's ice blue gown for her cousin's wedding. Elizabeth Bradford looked up from her handwork as her daughter settled herself across the room. "How was your evening with Roger, Louisa?" she asked. "Are you becoming serious about that young man? What about your relationship with Peter?"

"Roger and I are very good friends, Mother," Louisa said as she picked up her handwork. "He cares about me, and I enjoy our times together. Peter doesn't seem to care if I'm lonely. He never hints at when he'll return. I guess he expects me to enjoy a dull life. . .and be content with my embroidery. I'm not!"

"You are an adult, Louisa, and will make your own choices. But Roger doesn't seem interested in God or spiritual things. I truly believe he cannot be a Christian although he claims to be one. And the Bible cautions us not to be unequally yoked with an unbeliever."

"Mother! The Bible says we are not to judge one another!"

"I know, dear, but it also says in Matthew 7:20, 'By their fruits ye shall know them.' And we haven't seen any fruit in

Roger Evans's life, have we?"

"Well, usually he's kind and attentive and thoughtful. Isn't being kind a fruit of the spirit? If it weren't for Roger, I'd be living a pretty colorless life."

"I know waiting for Peter to return is hard, dear. But I trust you will pray about any decisions you make. Marriage is a serious matter."

There was that word again, "serious." It unnerved Louisa. "Oh, fiddle!" she exclaimed. "I guess I'm a fickle person, Mother! I'm sure that's what you and Father must think. And maybe I am fickle. I cared. . . ," she hesitated, "loved. . .Peter at one time. But he's gone and now I'm not sure about my feelings. Roger is here. I. . .I'm confused. I don't know who I care about anymore!"

During the following week, Elizabeth sewed furiously on the blue frock of satin and lace, so it would be finished in time for Clara's wedding the Saturday after Thanksgiving. Louisa saw Roger briefly at the bank several times before her family's departure for Augusta. Each time he seemed his old self again, and she felt warm and happy during their talks. Why did he have to be so charming at times? His amusing ways tugged at her heart.

The Jack and Phillip Bradford families enjoyed a joyful and blessed Thanksgiving together in Augusta. Elizabeth Bradford helped her sister-in-law with the food preparations while Louisa and Clara set the table in a festive manner. Much to Clara's delight, Sam Burns, her prospective bridegroom, joined the two families at their Thanksgiving feast. Phillip Bradford prayed over the food and thanked God for all His benefits. "Truly we are a blessed people," he said in conclusion, "and You are a great and mighty God."

The afternoon went quickly as they talked about the upcoming wedding. When they sang around the piano, Clara and Louisa took turns playing the accompaniment. Their voices rang out with the wonderful hymns of the faith. Louisa tried her best to be lighthearted and had completely fooled everyone except Clara.

Later that evening, after Sam left and the family retired, Clara faced her cousin and countered, "Something is wrong, Louisa. You wrote so gaily about your new friend, Roger Evans. What has happened to your love for Peter? Do you plan to break your engagement?"

Louisa's face clouded as she turned toward her cousin. "I've been a silly goose, Clara. Roger seemed so attentive and thoughtful, I've allowed myself to become involved. It's because I've been so lonely without Peter! I wondered if Roger might be the right one for me."

"What happened, dear cousin?" Clara asked.

"I must have encouraged Roger more than I realized because he asked me to elope with him. He insisted I pack a bag so we could leave immediately."

"Elope!" Clara gasped. "Why would he expect you to elope? Of course you want a church wedding with family and friends. Weddings are important to women."

"Not to Roger. He said a church wedding is ridiculous. When I told him an elopement was out of the question, he got angry."

"Well, I declare! Mr. Roger Evans seems uncaring about your feelings in the matter. I always thought the bride planned the wedding. Anyway, you plan to marry Peter, not Roger."

Louisa shook her head. "I told Peter in a letter I was seeing Roger and that he cared about me. I intimated that I enjoyed our outings. . .and wasn't sure what might happen in the future. What will he think of me now, Clara?"

❧

The Sam Burns, Clara Bradford wedding was a beautiful occasion. The church was filled to capacity with family and friends who witnessed the touching ceremony. Louisa walked down the aisle in her ice-blue frock followed by Clara on the arm of her father. Clara's gown, white satin trimmed with lace, boasted a fitted bodice. A crown of net and lace flowed out behind her from the golden head and a smile touched her mouth as she looked toward her bridegroom. Sam stood sedately at the altar with the pastor and his one attendant. His eyes, glued upon his bride, reflected love and tenderness. Louisa, misty-eyed but composed, sang two appropriate songs chosen by the couple. Her lyric soprano voice rang out pure and sweet over the hushed audience.

When Louisa returned to her position next to Clara, she felt a sense of joy as she surveyed the couple. There was no question about Clara and Sam's love for one another. For herself, Louisa felt unfulfilled. She longed to be a bride. Would she ever know the true joy of sharing her life with someone she loved? Or had she, by her foolish, fickle nature, ruined her one chance for happiness?

❧

Peter reflected on the days, which passed so quickly. Thanksgiving had come and gone and still no concrete news concerning his brother's crime. Several times, on visits to his brother, Genevieve Markam would be there, also. He realized more and more that she was a remarkable and devoted young woman. Sometimes Genny brought food for both him and his brother. The Thanksgiving meal was especially delicious, and the three of them had a time of fellowship and prayer together. Peter made it a habit to stay only a short time after Genny arrived, so the couple could be alone. He knew he would want privacy with his sweetheart if he were in Thomas's circumstances.

The week after Thanksgiving Peter received a letter from Annabelle. She wrote regularly, but this time she had enclosed a letter from Louisa. Peter's heart pounded within his chest when he saw her note. He tore open the sweet smelling envelope and took deep whiffs. A heady feeling enveloped him as he remembered the sweet scent of his darling Louisa when he held her in his arms. Within moments he had finished reading her message. It was a short note and aloof. A fierce pain shot through his heart and mind as he reread her words. She had found someone else! Another man had entered the picture—someone who cared about her. He could understand that. How could any man help but care about Louisa? She was such a warm, vibrant, beautiful person. But did this man really love her as Peter loved her? Were his intentions serious? Peter groaned outwardly as his eyes reread the words that cut him the most. "He really cares about me. I don't know what the future holds." The balance of Louisa's letter was cool and she signed it sincerely—not love.

"I've been away too long," Peter moaned as he crumpled the letter and threw it on the table. "But I thought we had something special between us, something that would last. We made a commitment to each other when we became engaged. Why did this happen with my brother just at this time, Lord? Thomas needed me, and I couldn't let him down. You knew I would want to see this thing through, show him I cared, and be his support. Not just for his sake, but for Annabelle's. I don't understand why these things happen. I know You have a purpose behind everything You allow to come into my life. I really messed up because I didn't tell Louisa the entire story. Because I love her, I didn't want to burden her with my troubles. It's my own fault she is enamored with another man. I thought Louisa loved me," Peter's voice choked as he mumbled the words, "as much as I love her." He pulled out his handkerchief and blew his nose. "There's no way I could be interested in another woman. . .not while I had Louisa." Peter thought about her laugh and the way her golden tresses framed her oval face. Her wide, gray eyes often sparkled with amusement, teasing him. Peter shook his head as though to clear his mind. "Help me to understand, Lord," he sighed. "I don't know the 'why' of it, and I don't need to, but this is a tough blow."

Peter tried to hide his grief as he set out to visit his brother that afternoon. He rode Thunder hard toward town as dust from the road flew up into his face. It didn't matter. He wanted to put Louisa out of his mind for the moment and center his thoughts on his brother's situation. He went first to his lawyer's office.

"What is taking so long?" he demanded. "It seems you are dragging your feet. Why aren't you out searching for leads?"

The lawyer, a short, stout man with spectacles, leaned back in his chair and eyed Peter. "You-all are in too much of a hurry," he drawled. "This kind of case takes time. We'll get you some answers soon enough."

"It's already too late for me!" Peter exclaimed. "I should have been out of here long ago!"

"Well now, Mr. McClough, don't you-all like our hospitality? We Southern folks pride ourselves on Southern hospitality."

"I do, Sir," Peter said with a softened tone. "You've all been most gracious. But I need to get my brother out of jail, if possible. And I need to get back north to my home. I have some personal matters to take care of. My entire future is at stake. It may be too late already!"

Halfheartedly, Peter left the lawyer's office and headed toward the jail. Genevieve Markam entered just ahead of him. Peter greeted her and allowed her to go back to speak with Thomas while he talked to the sheriff. The sheriff, always friendly, smiled as Peter approached.

"I have a lead on something, Peter, and it's about to be finalized. It will give us some answers. I hope they clear up this situation, one way or another."

Peter caught his breath. "What do you mean, Sheriff? What kind of answers? Will it help my brother's case?"

"I sincerely hope so. Regardless of the outcome, it will settle the case once and for all, and that is important."

"How soon?" Peter demanded. "Will it be today or tomorrow?"

"There are two people I must interview, so it may take a few days. I'm trying to line up a time when they will see me. They have agreed to tell me all they know. I just hope they don't back down on their word."

"But it sounds hopeful, doesn't it Sheriff? I'll pray about it along with my brother and Miss Markam. There is power in prayer, you know."

"Well, uh. . .we'll see. I've never been much on prayer. . . always worked things out by myself. Never felt I needed any help."

"Oh, but we do, Sheriff. We need God's help all the time. He's only a prayer away. He hears the prayers of His children, those who have trusted His Son, Jesus, as their Savior. God cares about us and every problem in our lives."

"What if we've never. . .uh. . .accepted His Son as our Savior? Does He still hear our prayers, Peter?"

"He hears the prayer of a repentant heart. I was once a lost sinner, Sheriff. Everyone is until they cry out to God as I did. The Bible is clear on that. Each person must confess he is a sinner and ask Jesus to come into his life."

"Wal. . .that's something I'd like to ponder for a while, Peter. But you-all go ahead and pray. It can't hurt none, and it sure will be interesting to see what happens."

Peter was optimistic as he shared the sheriff's news with Thomas and Genevieve. He needed, above all, to be an encouragement to the couple. He plastered a smile on his face to cover his own heartache. The smile didn't feel natural to him, but Thomas and Genevieve didn't seem to notice.

After a short visit and time of prayer, Peter took his leave promising to return the next day. He bought a few groceries and stopped by the barber for a haircut. As he mounted Thunder for the ride back, the animal seemed ready to get moving. "You're anxious to get back, aren't you, fella?" he whispered in the animal's ear. "I don't blame you. Powder is a beautiful mare. She's not fickle like women are. I'm sure she misses having you at her side." Thunder snorted and shook his head up and down as if to agree. Peter sighed audibly, gave the animal full rein, and let him ride at full gallop toward the plantation. The cool wind whipped color into his cheeks. He bent low over Thunder's back as the dust flew up from the roadway. It was exhilarating, and the cold air pushed thoughts of Louisa deep into the recesses of his mind.

Peter spent the afternoon cleaning the manure out of the barn. He spread fresh straw in the stalls, mended several loose boards, and oiled the saddles and harnesses. From there he went to the pasture and skirted the length and breadth of it. The horses trotted beside him and nuzzled him as he worked. Every so often he found a place that needed repair. He pounded almost fiercely in an attempt to ease the pain in his heart. When he finished his task, he saddled Powder to give her a run. They trotted around the pasture from one end to the other several times. Not to be left behind, Thunder followed at her side and stayed with them until they rode back to the barn. After Peter removed Powder's saddle and rubbed her down, Thunder whinnied and tossed his head. Powder responded with a whinny and the two of them raced off to the pasture. Peter watched them go. The dark stallion with the restless nature led the way, followed by the lovely and gentle bay mare. They jerked their heads, snorted to one another, and raced the length of the pasture before stopping to graze, side by side.

"Sometimes horses have more sense than humans," Peter muttered. "Look how they stay together. That's what I hoped for Louisa and me. To be together always. . .side by side."

That evening Peter prepared a letter for Annabelle.

Dear Annabelle,
I know it's been a long time, and I wish I knew when Thomas's case would be settled. The sheriff informed me today about two people who are willing to talk. It seems

*they have information about what happened that night at
the Berringer Plantation. Whether it will help Thomas
or convict him further, I do not know, but we must never
give up hope. Thomas, Genevieve, and I pray together
each day. You will love Genevieve. She is a sweet
Christian, and she and Thomas love one another. When
they marry, you will have her as a daughter. I know you
always wanted a daughter. And just think, a special
bonus! There will probably be grandchildren! What a
blessing that will be! I will keep you informed of the outcome of the men's testimony. Keep praying, dear
Annabelle and looking up.*

*Love,
Peter*

It was a short message, but it informed Annabelle of the
latest news. She would know something could happen in the
next few days. Peter pulled out another piece of paper and
started to write Louisa. He wrote a few lines, crumpled the
paper, and threw it on the floor. His second attempt turned
out to be another disaster. He crumpled it and tossed it aside.
After several unsuccessful attempts, Peter gave up. He wrung
his hands and mopped his brow. "What's the use?" he
shouted at the wall. "She's met someone else she cares
about! And here I sit in Tennessee! My hands are tied. I don't
even know when I'll get back to Waterville!" Peter leaned
forward and placed his head in his hands. "Oh, Louisa," he
murmured. "If you only knew how much I love you!"

fourteen

Louisa and her parents attended church with the Phillip Bradfords the morning after Clara's wedding. Clara and Sam had already left on their honeymoon, a trip to the coast, and would be gone for one week. Louisa, anxious to get home to Waterville, ate little of the tasty meal prepared by her aunt after the church service. Phillip Bradford loaded their luggage into his carriage and drove his brother's family to the station, a short distance across town. The cold, brisk air whipped color into their cheeks as the horses trotted along the snow-packed roads. Large snowflakes cascaded down from the heavens. They sifted and swirled as they lit on everything—houses, roadways, fences, and people. The effect was breathtaking as the pure, white snow covered every dingy corner and provided a clean covering.

When the family reached the train station, Louisa climbed down from the carriage and lifted her face toward the heavens. Large flakes tumbled down and clung to her warm wraps and eyelashes. She laughed and whirled around in sheer delight. "Isn't this beautiful, Mother?" she asked. "I love the way the snow covers ugly things and makes them pure and white. Doesn't the Bible say something about 'Wash me, and I shall be whiter than snow'? I'd like my life to be pure like that. I've been selfish and self-centered of late. I wrote Peter and told him I cared about someone else. It was such a cold and distant letter. Whatever must he think of me now?"

Elizabeth Bradford smiled at her daughter. While Jack Bradford went to take care of their luggage, the two women had an opportunity to talk. "Yes, the verse you quoted is from the Bible, Louisa. Psalm 51, verse 7. And about Peter.

I'm sure he felt pain when he read your note, but I believe Peter loves you. Does this mean you have decided Peter is the right one for you after all? What about Roger Evans?"

"I've been fickle, Mother. I admit it. Roger is handsome and charming. His attentiveness took my breath away. Against my better judgment, I allowed myself to become involved. But Roger is a controlling person. . .as you said. And he can't be a Christian. He doesn't care about my desires. Everything has to be his way, or he gets angry. I've seen another side of him of late. If we did marry, I'm not sure it would last. I want a marriage like you and Father have. . .one that endures."

Elizabeth hugged her daughter as the snowflakes continued to tumble down and lightly cover their bonnets. "It's good to hear you talk this way, dear. You've matured through your experience with Roger."

"I'm glad you and Father didn't give up on me. I was pretty hardheaded at times."

Jack Bradford, tickets in hand, rushed toward them somewhat out of breath. "It appears I missed out on some serious conversation between my two girls," he said. "Is there anything important I should know?"

Louisa smiled and glanced at her mother with a twinkle in her gray eyes. Elizabeth grinned, while an unspoken message passed between them. "Just girl talk, Jack," she said as she took her husband's arm and headed toward the train. "Just girl talk!"

Crowds of passengers thronged together as the engine spewed curls of dark smoke upward toward the heavens. The short, rotund conductor called "All Aboard!" loudly as he collected tickets from eager passengers pushing their way into the coaches. A sigh of relief escaped Louisa's lips as she settled into the seat beside her parents. It had been a busy, happy, yet exhausting few days in Augusta. A whirlwind of activities, including a bridal party at the church and a wedding rehearsal, had taxed everyone. Louisa knew her parents would doze on the trip home. She preferred instead to daydream about her own wedding, which she hoped would take place sometime in the near future. As she thought about Peter, she felt a deep pang of regret. He might consider her too fickle to be marriage material. Would he want to spend his entire life with someone so changeable, someone so childish? She wondered where he was, what he was thinking, and when he would return to Waterville. Eventually, she felt a wave of drowsiness wash over her, and she slept the balance of the way home.

ॐ

"I cannot understand it!" Jack Bradford said, an annoyed edge to his voice. "I told Roger exactly when we would arrive back in Waterville! The train is only fifteen minutes late. He should be here waiting to take us home."

"Perhaps he was delayed, Father," Louisa said, as she pulled her wraps closer about her body. "Roger is always working on something at the bank."

"Sometimes I wonder about that man," Jack exclaimed. "He's forever pulling out accounts and checking on them. There's no need for it. . .none at all!"

Elizabeth pulled on her husband's arm. "Let's go into the station and wait, dear. He'll be along in a bit. It's getting colder by the minute."

"Of course, Elizabeth. At least we have a warm place to wait. You and Louisa go on ahead. I'll locate our luggage and be right in. Roger will find us when he arrives."

The trio, alert since their naps on the train, sat close to the large, potbellied wood stove while they waited. Time passed slowly as Louisa watched, her eyes glued on the regulator clock on the far wall. *Tick-tock, tick-tock.* A half hour passed— then an hour. Passengers came and went, and still no Roger Evans appeared.

"Something's happened!" Jack said as he stood up. "We

can't wait any longer. I'll hire a carriage to take us home."

"Perhaps Roger is ill," Elizabeth said.

"He should have asked someone else to meet us," Jack said impatiently. "He appears to be a diligent worker most of the time, but he's lax in other areas. You'll probably think I have a suspicious mind, but sometimes I have doubts about his character."

❧

Before long, Jack hired a carriage and the trio started for home. He directed the coachman to make a stop at Roger's boardinghouse. "I'll only be a minute," Jack said as he climbed from the carriage. "I need to find out why Roger failed to show up. Perhaps he is ill and in need of a doctor."

Several minutes later Jack Bradford reappeared with furrowed brow, his lips drawn into a tight line. Without a word, he climbed into the carriage.

"Is it serious, Father?" Louisa asked. "How sick is Roger?"

Jack Bradford frowned. "No, he's not ill, Louisa. He's not sick at all."

Elizabeth turned to her husband. "What is it, Jack? Something is wrong. Your expression gives you away."

Jack Bradford sat stunned for a few moments as the coach carried them toward home. "He's gone," he muttered. "Roger Evans checked out of his boardinghouse, paid his rent, and left."

"Where did he move, Father? He's been looking at other places. Roger was never happy at the boardinghouse. He had fine ideas of a big home somewhere in the area."

"No. . .no. . .Louisa. . .nothing like that. He left no forwarding address. His landlady, Mrs. Hogan, said he moved out Friday and planned to leave town on the evening train. When she asked him where he was going, he said he wasn't sure of his plans. But he was through here in Waterville. He had finished with this town. He completed what he came to do."

"What can it mean, Jack?" Elizabeth asked. "He's through in Waterville. He finished what he came to do. It doesn't make sense, does it?"

"No sense at all," Jack muttered. "I don't have a clue as to what Roger meant. Do you know anything about this, Louisa? You were close to Roger."

"No, Father," she faltered. "I had no idea Roger planned to leave town. When we were together last week, Roger asked me to elope with him that same night."

Elizabeth gasped and caught her breath.

"But I refused," Louisa said quickly. "When Roger couldn't convince me to run off with him, he grew angry. I realized Roger had another side to his character, and I knew I could never marry anyone so changeable. . .attentive one moment and angry the next."

"Well, Louisa," her father muttered, "I'm glad you're not all enthralled with Roger. Your mother and I knew he was wrong for you from the start. We've prayed you would see that for yourself, and it seems you have." Jack Bradford sighed. "I wish I'd been more careful in selecting him as my assistant. He produced all the right records. His military service during the war seemed excellent, but I've had some strange, mixed feelings about him of late. He did his work well, so I found nothing to fault him on. Now, it seems he's left me in the lurch. I'll be doing double duty at the bank until I find another assistant."

"Could I help out, Father?" Louisa asked, a note of eagerness in her voice. "I feel so useless sometimes. I'm not in college anymore. I help Mother some with the house, but I'm tired of sitting home and working on embroidery. I've enough handwork stashed in my hope chest for two brides. And marriage seems out of the picture for me, at least at the present time. I could do some filing and handle some of the easier tasks at the bank. I did well in math. . .as far as I went with it. Could I help you out until you find another assistant?"

"Thanks," her father said absently. "I may take you up on it. You'd be an asset to the bank, my dear."

When they arrived at the Bradford home, Jack built a roaring fire in the large fireplace to ward off the chill. Elizabeth and Louisa prepared a light supper, and they carried it in by the fireside. The trio sat quietly for several moments as they watched the logs crackle and hiss. Elongated shadows stretched upward toward the ceiling and into other parts of the room. Louisa glanced sideways at her father. His eyes, glued on the fire, stared straight ahead. She noted the firm set of his jaw and furrowed brow. He wrung his hands, relaxed them, and wrung them again. Elizabeth reached for his hands and quieted them as she held them in her own. "Don't fret so, Jack. Everything will be all right at the bank. You've weathered difficult situations before."

Jack Bradford's face relaxed as he looked at his wife and daughter. "You are right, Elizabeth. We've had hard times in the past, but God always saw us through them."

"And He will again, dear," Elizabeth said.

Jack Bradford stared again at the fire for several moments, as if lost in thought. "I have a strange, uneasy feeling about Roger's sudden departure. He seemed edgy when he took us to the train station last Wednesday. Did you notice?"

"He was upset with me, Father, because I refused to elope with him," Louisa said. "I'm sure that was his problem."

Jack Bradford stroked his mustache thoughtfully. "No. . . no! I think it was more than that. I believe he planned his departure to coincide with our trip to Augusta. But I'll know the truth of the matter tomorrow when I open the bank. Perhaps he left a note of some kind or gave a message to one of the other employees. If he obtained a better position somewhere, he should have confided in me. I'm not an unreasonable person. I could have given him references and prepared for his resignation." Jack Bradford sighed heavily and stood to his feet. "Let's join hands and have a word of prayer before we retire. I want to turn this entire situation over to the Lord. He is our helper and comfort in times of trouble."

fifteen

The following day winds howled as they blew in a nor'easter. Snow no longer drifted down in soft flakes. Instead it blew almost horizontally as the winds gusted and swirled. Jack Bradford arose early, but Louisa was up and dressed ahead of him.

"Breakfast is ready, Father," she said. "And I'm going with you to the bank this morning. Mother agrees with me. You need some support, and I'm prepared to do whatever I can to help out."

"But Louisa, I don't even have the facts of the whole matter yet. Perhaps Roger will show up as usual, and all will be a misunderstanding. His landlady may have misunderstood Roger's intentions."

"That could be so, Father. But I intend to accompany you in the event he doesn't show up. I'm sure there are many things I can do to lighten the workload. In fact, I'm looking forward to it. It's about time I made myself useful and learned something about the banking business."

Jack Bradford looked from his daughter to his wife as a crooked smile tugged at his mouth. "Clearly I am outnumbered. I can see my wife and daughter have already made their decision. Elizabeth, if you want Louisa to go with me, I will not argue the matter. Perhaps it is indeed time for our daughter to learn how the family business operates. After all, the bank will be included in her inheritance."

Louisa's gray eyes sparkled, and she bubbled with excitement as she wrapped her arms around her father's neck. "Oh, thank you, Father!" It was a new adventure for her, and she welcomed the challenge.

After breakfast Louisa and her father set out for the bank, bundled warmly against the north wind. It whipped at their faces and Louisa pulled her warm, wool bonnet farther down over the golden curls. It was a relief when they arrived at the bank and were able to escape the cold blast of the nor'easter in all its fury. Mr. Bradford started the wood stove and soon they were able to remove their outer wraps. He searched the office and front desk, but there was no note from Roger Evans. When he checked the vault, his countenance sank. Louisa heard her father gasp and mumble, "Oh, no! It can't be!"

Louisa peered into the open vault. Her father's face paled as he wrung his hands. Louisa clutched his arm. "What happened Father? Has someone tampered with the vault?"

Jack Bradford looked at his daughter through glazed eyes. Blindly he brushed a hand across his forehead as if to clear his vision. "It's all gone. The people's money. . .thousands of dollars. . .it's been stolen. I. . .I must tell the authorities immediately. Perhaps they can trace him. . .wherever he's gone. Dear God, I pray they can catch up with him."

"Who, Father? Who would do such a thing? Surely not Roger Evans. I found him self-centered and controlling, but surely he wouldn't stoop to this."

"Roger is the only one who could have done this, Louisa. No other person has access to the vault. And no one else knows the extent of the money stored there. Roger studied the accounts. He knew everything about our business here at the bank. Perhaps that's what he meant when he told his landlady he was through in Waterville. He had finished here. Roger may have a record of thievery, going from one place to another." Jack Bradford shook his head. "He seemed so sincere, so honest. His papers. . .records. . .seemed to be in order. And he told me he served in the Union army during the Civil War. That carried a lot of clout with me. I like to give employment to our men who served so faithfully. Everything Roger showed me must have been a forgery. How could I have been such a poor judge of character?"

"Father, I'm so sorry. Don't blame yourself too much. Roger Evans is a smooth character. He fooled you and me, and I'm sure he fooled others. When you hired him, you believed he was an upright and moral person. Evidently he is not."

Jack Bradford put on his hat, boots, and pulled his warm wraps around him. "I must go to the authorities, Louisa. You wait here, and I'll return as soon as I give them an account of the robbery. When my other two employees arrive, tell them the bank will be closed today and send them home. Don't give them any details about what happened. Tell them I'll stop by and explain everything to them later. They may have a clue to all this. I don't want to cause a panic among the people. The sheriff will know what to do. He'll want to question my employees, I'm sure. And he'll need a description of Roger before he can get the word out. Let's hope Roger Evans hasn't skipped the country."

Louisa busied herself in her father's absence. She found a cloth and dusted the counters and desks. Using a broom stored in a back closet, she swept the floor and tried to neaten the place. When her father's employees arrived, she told them the bank would be closed for the day. She also shared the fact that her father would visit their home later and explain the situation. The employees, though puzzled over the circumstances, asked no questions and took their leave.

The bank was closed for an entire week, which made a hardship on some. The Bradfords discovered Roger Evans was indeed a thief. He had embezzled monies before in various banks across the country and was wanted by the authorities. He never stayed longer than a few months in one place as he moved around from one state to another. Louisa gasped and clutched her throat when she learned he had several wives and a few children in various locations. If she had agreed to run off and elope with him, she would be counted as one of the unfortunate women. Thus far Roger Evans had escaped the law and continued his renegade lifestyle. There were few clues to go on, but one of Jack Bradford's employees had a bit of news. One week earlier he overheard Roger talking to one of the customers regarding Maine's frigid temperatures. The employee remembered Roger's comments word for word. "I'm not a Northerner at heart, Ma'am. The weather in Florida is most appealing to me at this time of year." Whether the comment had any bearing on the case, only time would tell.

Phillip Bradford, Jack's brother, advanced him monies, so the Waterville bank could get back in business. The people of Waterville, for the most part, were understanding about the delay. It took time for the authorities to track Roger Evans's route from the time he left Waterville. They found he had taken the Kennebec Train out of Waterville to Portland. From there they drew a blank, as there was no record of anyone securing a ticket under the name of Roger Evans. However, they knew he changed his name often—every time he hit a bank or business in a different state. Obviously he had changed it again. This made it difficult for the police, but they were dedicated to their task. Roger Evans, alias several other names, needed to be brought to trial and pay for his crimes.

Louisa went to the bank each day with her father and helped file records and fill in at the counter. She not only enjoyed the work, she brightened the atmosphere. When Louisa greeted customers, she always flashed her cheerful smile. Her father often praised her saying he wondered why he hadn't brought her into the bank earlier. She needed to learn the business, he told her, in the event anything happened to him, especially since he had no son or son-in-law to carry on the work at the bank. And anyway, he had confessed, he enjoyed her company. Louisa knew that in his earlier years,

Jack Bradford longed for a son with a passion. But the good Lord had not seen fit to bless her parents with other children, and they had accepted the fact that God knows what He is doing and does all things well.

Louisa's cheerful attitude did not reach her heart. Deep down she wondered about Peter. There had been no more letters, and she hungered for one. Her short infatuation with Roger Evans was a mistake. He had flooded her with attention, and she was ripe for it. She had a lot of time to think, and the more she thought about Peter, the more she missed him. Visions of his dark hair and the way a shock of it fell across his forehead crowded her mind. She longed to tease him and hear his hearty laugh as he reached for her. His dark eyes and tender glances always took her breath away. When he took her in his arms, she leaned against his shoulder and his manly scent filled every fiber of her being. "Foolish girl," she whispered to herself. "You gave up your handsome prince, and now you have no one!"

The days passed slowly for Louisa. She kept her mind occupied by serving at the bank, but each afternoon she looked for a letter from Peter. As the weeks came and went without a letter, she became depressed. *What kept him away from Waterville so long?* she wondered. She saw Martha, his part-time housekeeper, occasionally at the bank. But Martha had no news to tell her except what she already knew. Peter had business to take care of and would return as soon as it was finished. With this she must be content.

The Christmas season brightened Louisa's thoughts as she helped her mother decorate the house for the holidays. A special wreath topped with miniature bells and a cranberry velvet bow adorned the front door. Garlands and boughs dressed the fireplace mantle interspersed with tiny candles. Bright velvet bows, placed here and there among the boughs, lent a festive appearance. The staircase, also embellished with garlands and bows, displayed a brass candlestick on each step going to the second floor.

On a Saturday afternoon, Louisa and her parents took the sleigh and set out for the farm of her friend Emily's parents. The Masons had given them a standing invitation to cut their Christmas tree from their woods each year. Louisa remembered how, as a child, her father carried her on his shoulders as they tramped through knee-deep snow to find just the right tree. With the tree tied to the back of their sleigh, Louisa and her parents sang Christmas carols on the way home. It lifted their spirits as they sang the familiar songs. Their voices rang out clear and strong in the cold, crisp air. Worries and cares seemed of no consequence as they rejoiced in the beauty of the season.

The authorities had various clues but had not yet located Roger Evans or the stolen money. Jack Bradford's bank was out of the red and doing well. It was only possible, however, due to the generosity of Phillip Bradford. Jack was deeply indebted to his brother, and Louisa knew the situation bothered him. Would his financial situation be cleared up soon, so he could pay his brother back?

Louisa's concerns often turned to Peter. Her mind lingered on her memories of him. Would he come back to Waterville in time for Christmas? And if he did, would he want to see her? Her only letter to him, in all this time, intimated she cared for someone else. Should she write him again and explain what a foolish goose she had been? He hadn't written since he received her letter about Roger. Perhaps he had found a new love. Someone beautiful—someone who appreciated him— someone who wasn't so fickle. Maybe Peter McClough had written her off—and could never care for her again.

Louisa sang louder as she pushed these thoughts from her mind. Her sweet soprano voice echoed across the countryside as the horses clip-clopped along the roadway toward home. It was the Christmas season and the beautiful message of "Silent Night, Holy Night" filled her heart with unspeakable joy.

sixteen

Peter McClough battled inner feelings of depression as he waited for answers regarding his brother's trial. It was the week before Christmas, and he longed to be back home. When he left so hastily back in September, it never occurred to him he would be gone such a long time. He knew Martha, his part-time housekeeper, looked after his house. She had written him on several occasions to assure him all was well. Her letters, written in care of Annabelle, had been forwarded to Tennessee.

Louisa had written no further letters, nor had he written any to her. Perhaps she and this other man, Roger Evans, were even married by this time. The thought caused Peter much pain, and he drew a hand across his brow as he pushed back the shock of dark hair from his forehead. Gloomily he glanced out the window and prepared for his daily trip into town. The skies, dark with ominous clouds, matched his emotions. "Surely the sheriff will get this thing settled before Christmas," he muttered. "I dread to think of Thomas sitting in that jailhouse during the holidays. This is the time we celebrate the birthday of our King. It should be a joyous time of remembrance." The frown left his face, and a shadow of a smile lit the corners of his mouth.

"Forgive me, Lord, for looking on the downside of everything. I will keep looking up!" Peter finished dressing, ate a light breakfast, and did a few chores. When he saddled Powder for his ride into town, Thunder threw back his dark head and nickered. "It's all right, boy! We'll only be gone a short time. I'll bring Powder back." Thunder seemed to understand for he nuzzled Peter and let him run his hand through the thick, black mane. It was a leisurely trip into

Nashville until winds blew in a cold rain from the north. Peter drew his slicker closer around him as Powder rode at full gallop the remainder of the way. When he entered the jailhouse, he noticed two strangers seated with the sheriff. The sheriff smiled, reached out a hand to Peter, and pointed toward a chair.

"What's up, Sheriff?" Peter asked. "Do these men have any bearing on Thomas's case?"

"Yes, they do," the sheriff drawled. "I've waited a long time for them to be willing to testify. They were concerned about retribution from the Klan, but they've agreed to tell what they know. I've convinced them they have a debt of responsibility here. Your brother's life is at stake."

The sheriff introduced Peter to the two men who had taken on assumed names to protect their identity. They stood up and reached to shake hands with Peter. Their furrowed brows and tightly drawn lips lent an air of emotional strain.

Peter shook their hands warmly. "Thank you for coming forth with your testimony!" he exclaimed. "I appreciate any information you can give us about the killings. I hope it will help my brother's situation. But whether it does or not, we need to know the truth of the matter."

"Judge Barnhouse will hear the case at the courthouse this afternoon," the sheriff said. "Promptly at one o'clock. Miss Markam plans to be in attendance, and it is open to the public. These gentlemen will give their testimony then, under oath. Thomas will also relate his story of what happened at the Berringer Plantation. What occurred was tragic and senseless. We'll have some answers for you today, Peter. This situation has gone on long enough. It's time to clear the air one way or another."

Peter spent the balance of the morning in conversation with his brother. He encouraged Thomas to hope for a quick settlement in the case, one that would be in his favor.

"I don't know how it can be in my favor, Peter. Facts are

facts." Thomas drew a hand across his eyes as if to blot out the memory of that fateful night. "It was a heinous crime. They hung Ben on a tree at the back of the house. He must have been already dead when I arrived because he didn't make a sound. . .he just hung there swinging from the rope. His cabin was enveloped in flames and past any hope of saving the house or his family. I was so angry I lost my head. I shouted at the men, but they jumped on their horses and rode away. When I fired my rifle at them, one of the Klansmen fell to the ground. After I took Ben down from the tree, I. . .I. . ." Thomas looked at his brother with moist, reddened eyes. "Ben was dead, Peter! My best friend was dead! I went over to the man I'd shot later. He was dead, also. But you know all this. After I buried Ben, his family, and the Klansman, I left and went north to see Annabelle. My state of mind was desperate."

Peter agonized with his brother. His own troubles seemed unimportant compared to the hurt and pain Thomas experienced. "It had to be a terrible thing to witness. I'm sure I would have reacted in the same way. Hopefully the judge will take the entire story into consideration."

Though his eyes were still moist, a slight smile crossed Thomas's face. "You are a good brother, Peter, and a dear friend. I appreciate you more every day. You've been away from home for three months and never complained. I know you miss Louisa. You talked of her so often when you first arrived. Lately you haven't mentioned her, but I know you are anxious to get back to Waterville where your sweetheart lives. Let's hope this case gets settled today."

At noon Peter went to the small cafe on Main Street and brought back a lunch meal for the two of them. Then the brothers had a time of fellowship and prayer. They committed the outcome of the trial to the Lord and left it completely in His hands. Peter's heart felt lighter as he left the jailhouse and stopped by his lawyer's office for a brief meeting. The lawyer sounded optimistic about the case and felt Thomas had a good chance for a light sentence.

As Peter walked to the courthouse for the one o'clock session, he pondered what the outcome would be. Due to the circumstances of the situation, could Thomas receive a short jail sentence rather than a lengthy one? He refused to consider a death sentence. Surely the judge would never allow that to happen. And the two men in the sheriff's office. What testimony could they share that might have a bearing on the case? Peter quickened his step, entered the courthouse, and took a seat in the second row directly behind his brother.

❧

The judge, an austere looking man in his fifties, sat at a desk at the front. His long robe, gray hair, and thick spectacles added to the prestige of his office. A clerk sat directly in front and to the right of him, prepared to write down the course of action during the trial. The judge called Thomas to the witness stand first and he related his story, word for word, as it happened.

"Where was the Klansman when you shot him?" the judge asked.

"He was riding away on horseback, Your Honor."

"Was he facing you?"

"No, Sir. There was a group of them, and they were leaving in a hurry. I'm sorry to say I shot him in the back."

"Are you certain of that? Perhaps the man turned around toward you."

"No, Sir. I fired at his back, and he fell to the ground. Then I went to get my friend down from the tree. I dragged him several feet away from the area, but he was already dead. It. . .it was very painful for me." Thomas pulled out his bandana and wiped the moisture from his face before he continued. "I located a good burial spot out in back and buried him and his family. Then I went over to find the Klansman. His horse had run off. The man lay on his stomach. . .dead also. So I dragged him back to the burial grounds."

"And you buried the man along with your friends in a little burial plot, is that right?"

"Yes Sir, I did. I thought it the right thing to do. I marked the graves of my friend and his family, but the man's grave was left unmarked. When I came back in September to turn myself in, the grave was empty."

"I see," the judge said as he glanced at some papers in front of him. "The body had been removed from the grave sometime earlier. That agrees with information I have. You may step down Mr. Hayes."

Thomas's lawyer gave a brief account of his client's deep sorrow over what had occurred. He reminded the judge that Thomas Hayes returned to the area by his own free will and turned himself in to the sheriff. "This fact needs to be taken into consideration, Your Honor."

"I believe our sheriff has two men who are here to enlighten us regarding this case," the judge replied. "I'll hear their testimony before I pass any judgment on your client."

Thomas sat in the first row with his lawyer with Peter just behind them. The first of the two men to give testimony moved forward and was sworn in. Peter tapped his brother on the shoulder and comforted him with a smile of encouragement. Thomas's face, tense and drawn, relaxed somewhat as he leaned forward to listen to the man speak.

The first man's testimony startled the judge and the many people seated at the trial. He revealed the fact he had been one of the Klansmen at the Berringer Plantation on the night of the murders. Shortly thereafter he left the society because he could not continue in their evil practices. "What I am about to say," he said, "is true. I say so before God and all who are present in this building. This man," he pointed at Thomas Hayes, "is not the murderer of my fellow Klansman."

There were several gasps in the audience as people shuffled their feet and turned in their seats. Loud murmuring issued forth until the judge ordered them to be quiet. Then he glanced at the witness and asked him to continue.

"There were about twelve of us gathered outside of town that fateful night. We knew Mr. Hayes was away, and the black folk were alone. Clay Prescott agreed to join the Klan one last time. He insisted this would be his final escapade with the group. He said he wanted nothing more to do with them from that night on. When the group heard this, they became angry and tried to dissuade him. But Clay Prescott could not be convinced to change his mind.

"The men shouted and worked themselves into a frenzy as they galloped hard toward the plantation. You may not believe this, but Clay and I hung back. We were there. . .we were in on it. . .but we only observed." The witness hung his head and wiped large beads of sweat from his brow. "Others grabbed the black man and set fire to his cabin, with the family in it asleep. Then they strung the black man up by the neck with a heavy rope and watched as he swung back and forth." The witness broke down and sobbed openly. He blew his nose loudly and struggled to continue. "That's when Mr. Hayes rode up and yelled at us. We rode off in a fury toward the woods. Clay and I were at the back of the group. I heard the rifle shot and saw Clay was hit in the back. But he stayed on his horse. One of the Klansmen turned toward him and shot him in the chest with a pistol at close range. I can honestly say I don't know which Klansman did this terrible thing. But that is when Clay fell from his horse, and I'm positive that is when he died."

There was another murmuring and moving about among the audience. "How can that be?" someone shouted. "Mr. Hayes said nothing about hearing a shot. He admits shooting Clay Prescott in the back. Let him pay for his crime!"

After the judge quieted the courtroom, he asked the witness the same question. "Mr. Hayes mentioned nothing about another shot. Why is that?"

"There could be several reasons," the witness said. "He

was some distance away. He was concerned about his friend and his friend's family. The cabin fire was a roaring blaze, crackling and hissing while timbers fell all around the place. Maybe one of the crashing pieces of timber muffled the sound."

The judge directed a question to Thomas. "Mr. Hayes, did you examine the body before you buried it? Surely you would have noticed if there were two shots in the victim's body."

"Your Honor, I assumed I had killed the man, so I did not examine his body. He was over toward the woods, face down, where it was very dark. I dug five graves and buried my friends. Then I dragged the man's body over to the small burial place."

The first witness stepped down and the other witness took his place. After being sworn in, he revealed his information. "I'm the one who dug up the deceased for the family and prepared him for a proper burial," he said. "The wound received from Mr. Hayes' rifle was in Clay Prescott's back, high near the right shoulder. It could not have killed him. He had a pistol wound in the chest near his heart. I'm certain this wound is the one which caused his death."

Some of the audience jumped up and caused a disturbance. People moved about while loud murmurs and shouts filled the air. The judge ordered them to be quiet and cleared the courtroom of all onlookers except witnesses, the sheriff, lawyers, and family. Genevieve Markam sat with her mother and dabbed at her eyes with her handkerchief. She looked across the aisle at Peter and whispered, "Thank God!"

Peter clapped his brother on the back. "I knew it would turn out for good, brother. God was on our side!"

The judge cleared his throat and stood up. "Ahem! I haven't made a decision on this case as yet." Everything was quiet as all eyes turned upon the man. Peter held his breath as he focused on the judge.

"I've listened to all the evidence, and it appears to be in order," the judge said. "These two witnesses should have come forward sooner. They withheld important information. I'm convinced they were reluctant due to fear of retribution from the Klan. Do you wish to push charges against them, Mr. Hayes?"

Thomas rose quickly to his feet. "No, Your Honor, I do not. I thank them personally for the strength of character to come forward with the truth at this time. It was a brave thing to do under the circumstances."

"Then I proclaim Thomas Hayes innocent of charges and free to go," the judge stated as he pounded his gavel. "It appears we do not know the identity of the Klansman who murdered Clay Prescott. His murder will remain unsolved unless further evidence is provided."

Those who remained rejoiced as they crowded around Thomas, slapping him on the back and shaking his hand. When Genevieve Markam approached, the others moved away. She walked boldly into his arms. Thomas drew her close and buried his head in the long, chestnut tresses. And Peter's heart ached for Louisa.

seVenteen

"You can't leave now, Peter!" Thomas exclaimed. "I need you here for the wedding. You will be my best man!"

The two brothers sat around the breakfast table the following morning and devoured a mound of pancakes. They had returned to the plantation the night before, after a supper meal with Genny and her mother. Anxious to get back to his house after the lengthy time in jail, Thomas borrowed a horse from the Markams's stable. He knew it would be too heavy a load for Powder to carry the two men back to the plantation.

"Anyway," Thomas continued, "I'm just getting used to having a brother. Why not move down here and help me run the place? After your marriage, you and Louisa could live here with Genny and me. This house is too big for us. When I get my cattle delivered, I'll need help. I'll hire some extra hands, but I'd like you to join me. What do you say, brother?"

Peter wiped his mouth with his napkin and stared at his plate. "Thanks for the offer, Thomas, but you and Genny need to be alone after your marriage. Three of us together in this house would be a crowd."

"Three of us!" Thomas exploded. "I mean the two couples. . . Genny, me, you, Louisa!"

Peter frowned as he faced his brother. "Louisa wrote me some time ago that she was seeing someone else. She could be married by this time."

"But you said nothing! Why didn't you tell me? I'm so sorry. All I've thought about was myself. I never knew you were hurting."

"Thomas, you had enough on your mind. I refused to burden you. Getting your trial over with was important. Now, you can

146

get on with your life. You and Genny can be married as planned. I'm happy for you both." Peter's mouth formed a crooked grin "But I will stay for the wedding. I'd like to share in your happiness. And I needn't hurry back to Waterville. If Louisa is already married, it will be painful for me."

Thomas eyed his brother, brows furrowed. "It's because of me, isn't it? Louisa got tired of waiting for you to come back. That's it, right?"

"Louisa knows nothing about you, Thomas. I left Waterville hurriedly when I got Annabelle's wire. Louisa only knows I had business to attend to and would be back when I completed it. If she really loved me, she should have been willing to wait. It's better this way, I guess. I love her more than I can say. But if she doesn't love me enough. . ." His voice broke and he continued huskily, "If she doesn't love me enough, then yes, it's better this way."

That afternoon, Thomas sent Annabelle a wire and asked her to come down for Christmas and the wedding, which would be celebrated two days later, and said he hoped she would stay on with them, at least for a while. The two brothers worked diligently getting the house ready for Thomas's bride and Annabelle's visit. Although they had little time to prepare, Genevieve and her mother took care of the details for the wedding. Genny had purchased her dress several months earlier when she and Thomas had become engaged.

Peter and Thomas checked out the pastures, secured several head of cattle, and more horses. They put up a Christmas tree and put forth their best efforts in decorating the tree and house for the holidays. As they stood back to survey their handiwork, they decided it passed inspection.

"Doesn't look too bad for a couple of bachelors," Thomas said as he handed Peter the angel for the top of the tree. "We almost forgot the traditional angel, though, and that's important. It will be wonderful to have a woman's touch on this place. Maybe Annabelle can pretty the house up a bit before the wedding. . .you know. . .feminine touches and such."

"Annabelle will love doing it, Thomas. And her cooking is something else, isn't it? It will be great to taste one of her home cooked-meals again."

Annabelle Hayes arrived two days before Christmas. Her round face and merry little laugh were a welcome sight. She hugged each of them in turn. "I'm so happy, Thomas," she said. "God answered our prayers and brought you through this terrible situation. And Peter, I don't know what we'd have done without you."

The two men gave Annabelle a tour of the house, and she oohed and aahed over the large home as she walked through one room after another. Once settled in one of the lovely bedrooms upstairs, she made her way to the kitchen where she felt most at home. Before long, the brothers sniffed tantalizing odors coming from the cook stove.

Annabelle insisted on preparing Christmas dinner. Mrs. Markam and Genny were invited, and it proved to be a festive occasion. They all talked at great length about the wedding and future plans of the couple. Although Thomas assured Mrs. Markam she was welcome to move in with him and Genny, she said she had made other arrangements. She planned to sell her large home and move in with her widowed sister. "Actually we'll have a jolly time together, and I'll still be close enough to visit you and Genny."

❧

After a short honeymoon, Thomas and Genny returned to the large plantation and settled in. Genny had ideas and suggestions for some feminine touches in the large house and was anxious to put them into action. "I have so many little things I'd like to add to this lovely home," she said in her sweet Southern drawl. "And Thomas promised me I could let my imagination run wild. . .with certain fabrics and candelabra. It will be delightful fun to make a few changes here and there."

Thomas asked Annabelle to make her home with them. Genevieve agreed with the suggestion and begged her to stay. "Since my mother won't be with us, I'll need some help, Annabelle. I don't think I can run this big house by myself. Thomas has promised me domestic help, but I'd like you here to oversee everything. Please tell me you'll stay. You were Thomas's mother for the first ten years of his life, and he's missed out on so much time with you. It would please us both if you would become a part of our family."

Annabelle flushed and her round face broke into a wide grin. Her merry little laugh echoed forth as she looked at them with loving eyes. "I appreciate your kind offer, Genny. There's nothing I'd like better than to live here with you and Thomas. There are some things I must take care of back in Boston first. But if you're sure I won't be in the way, I'd love to return and look after the two of you."

"Annabelle," Thomas said with emotion, "we'd like nothing better!"

"What about your little cottage, Annabelle?" Peter asked. "Do you plan to sell it?"

"I don't want to sell it, but I would like to turn it over to the little church. They could keep up the place and use it for visiting pastors or missionaries. Maybe even folk needing a place to stay from time to time. It would give me great pleasure to have it used by the Lord's people. The pastor and church folk have been so good to me over these many years."

"But what about your furniture and things, Annabelle?" Peter asked. "I'll need to help you pack everything and get it to the train."

"Only a few things, Peter. I'll leave the furniture for the new occupants. I have some smaller objects and keepsakes I won't part with. They carry a lot of memories and mean a great deal to me. And I didn't bring all my clothes with me. When we return to Boston, you can crate up my things for me. And we'll visit the cemetery so I can say good-bye to

Thomas. Oh, I know he isn't really there. It's just his body in that little plot of ground. His spirit is with the Lord. But I'll miss caring for his grave and tending the flowers. It's such a peaceful spot, and I feel close to him there." Annabelle's eyes misted over, and her lips quivered.

Peter put an arm around the fleshy body and gave her a gentle hug. "Your husband would want you to be with young Thomas and his bride, Annabelle. That way you won't be alone anymore. It sounds like the perfect situation for you. And when I come back to Tennessee for a visit, I'll be able to see you, also."

"Then it's all settled!" Thomas cried as he and Genny hugged Annabelle. "And I liked the way you admitted you would visit us, brother. We'll look forward to many visits from you in the future!"

"Of course I'll be back," Peter said with a mischievous grin. "I plan to leave Thunder with you. He likes it here, and you have plenty of pasture room for him. In town where I live. . .that's no place for a magnificent animal like Thunder. I'll be back to see my horse!"

"Great!" Thomas exclaimed with a chuckle, an arm around his bride. "That piece of horseflesh will be missed more than your own brother! I guess that tells me who is most important around here!"

Peter and Annabelle stayed on with Thomas and Genevieve for another week to help get the plantation restored to its full productive activity. When Peter and Annabelle said their good-byes, it was a touching farewell at the train station in Nashville. They all knew Annabelle would return soon and take up residency with them, but no one knew when Peter would return—not even Peter himself. The two brothers, with moist eyes and a catch in their throats, embraced unashamedly. "Just when I've found you, I'm losing you," Thomas said hoarsely. "We work so well together. I wish you could stay longer and help me run the place. It would be a shared partnership. . .the way I planned to do it with Ben."

"I'll be back, Thomas," Peter muttered as he pulled out his handkerchief and blew his nose. "That's a promise. And it may be sooner than you think."

Peter helped Annabelle onto the train, and they settled themselves toward the back of the coach. Annabelle took her handwork out of her bag and commenced to embroider the fine fabric as the train hastened down the tracks, belching and spitting smoke and steam. Peter leaned back and listened to the *clickety-clack, clickety-clack,* of the heavy wheels on the rails. He was bone tired from all the exertion during the past two weeks and longed to sleep. But his mind dwelt on thoughts of Louisa. He visualized her sweet oval face with the softly curved lips, her gray eyes so often wide in wonderment, and her charming innocence as she laid her golden head on his shoulder. How he longed to take her in his arms and never let her go. It pained him deeply to remember she cared about someone else and could be married by now. His face drew into a scowl at the thought. Perhaps she'd had a Christmas wedding, just as Thomas and Genevieve had. She would belong to another then and could never be his. Peter groaned aloud as he tried to put these disturbing thoughts from his mind.

"What's wrong, Peter?" Annabelle asked turning toward him, uneasy concern lining her face. "Does your body ache from all the hard work you were involved in at the estate? You worked such long hours. Your determination is commendable, but now I expect you are paying for it with sore muscles."

Peter looked into his cousin's eyes and reached to pat her round cheeks. "Annabelle, you seem more like a mother to me than a distant cousin. I appreciate your concern. I had the best laid plans for my life before I got your telegram last September. My lifestyle had changed when I became a Christian. I planned to follow the Lord wherever He led me, marry Louisa, and raise a family. Everything planned out! But I don't ache from the hard work at the plantation. In fact, I relished it. It kept me busy and my mind occupied. Now, when I have time on my hands, I think about Louisa more than ever. The fact that she might be married to someone else pains me. The ache I feel isn't in my muscles. It's in my heart!"

"I understand," Annabelle said softly. "You love Louisa with all your heart. After God, she is the dearest person in your life. I will pray about this situation, Peter."

"Thanks, prayer partner! I feel better knowing you are praying, too."

"Peter," Annabelle said thoughtfully as she stuck her needle into her handwork once again. "I am honored you think of me more as a mother than a distant cousin. It would be a privilege to have a dear son like you. As long as I live, I will pray for you and help you in any way I can."

❧

Jack and Elizabeth Bradford noted a decided change in their daughter. Louisa had matured into a caring, helpful, young woman. Her time at the bank proved her ability to buckle down and put her shoulder to the wheel. The days were no longer filled simply with long hours spent doing handwork or joining her mother at teas. It had given her a sense of worth and accomplishment. Her parents delighted in the new Louisa. Her thoughts, once self-centered and childish, were no longer for herself. After a day's work at the bank, she often visited a widow or shut-in from church and took them some broth or small cakes. The ladies welcomed her visits and enjoyed her fellowship. Louisa intended to brighten their lives and encourage their hearts. Often, after her conversations with these dear ones, she came away with the greater blessing.

She still cared about Peter, but kept her inner feelings to herself. It had been a mistake—a huge blunder—falling for Roger Evans who proved to be a no-good renegade. And she had no one to blame but herself. Her parents' warnings had gone unheeded. The letter written to Peter told him of her relationship with Roger. That was the reason he had not written again. Why should he? Her letter, cold and uncaring, left him no alternative. He had resigned himself to the fact she cared for someone else. Louisa shuddered as she considered Peter's reaction to the news. She bit her lip and denounced her cruel actions. Surely Peter could never care for her again!

Christmas came and went quietly at the Bradford home. It was a meaningful time with special church services, concerts, and visits with friends. During this time, Louisa grew in her Christian faith. The birth of the Savior and His eventual death on the cross gave new meaning to her life. Quiet times spent in Bible study and prayer provided her with a peace she had never experienced before. Oh, how much she had missed by living a nominal Christian life instead of feasting on the Scriptures and applying them to her life. She sought out passages in the New Testament and Psalms and committed them to memory. They became a great comfort to her.

In mid-January, the full blast of Maine's winter was at its height. Gales from the nor'easters brought in two feet of snow and left the Waterville residents snowbound. All activity came to a standstill. Eventually men with horses and plows managed to pile the huge mounds of white snow along the sides of the main streets. Louisa, anxious to get back to work at the bank after being confined for a few days, bundled herself warmly against the chill. She felt the cold air as it whipped at her cheeks and pulled at her clothing. Snow stuck to her eyelashes as she bent her head low against the wind for protection. Her father had left earlier in the day but insisted she wait and come in later. "There won't be many customers out today after this storm, Louisa," he had said. "Wait until I get the bank warmed up. The temperature in the rooms will be frigid until I heat up the wood stoves."

That afternoon a gentleman from the police investigation committee appeared and asked for Mr. Bradford. The man was plainly clothed in a dark suit rather than a police uniform. His small beady eyes peered through heavy spectacles as he fumbled with papers he lifted from his briefcase. "I'm J. D. Hackman here to see Mr. Bradford," he said in a hurried tone. "I hope he's in for I have some news for him regarding the theft here at the bank."

"Yes, Mr. Hackman," Louisa answered. "My father is in, and I'll tell him you are here." Excitement mounted in her chest as she headed toward her father's office. J. D. Hackman followed close behind her and almost bumped into her when she stopped at her father's office door. "I'm sorry, Miss. . . but I have urgent news for Mr. Bradford!"

"Well, come right on in, Sir," Louisa said as she opened the door. Jack Bradford sat at his desk going over some bank statements and looked up as they entered. "Father, this is Mr. Hackman," Louisa said. "He has important news for you about the bank robbery."

Jack Bradford stood up and extended his hand to the police investigator. "I hope it's good news, Mr. Hackman. We've been waiting for a break in this case for a long time. Please sit down and tell me what has happened so far."

J. D. Hackman settled his large frame into a chair close to Jack Bradford's desk. He leaned forward and spread some papers out in front of him. Tapping his fingers lightly, he pointed to some words written on one of the papers. Louisa held her breath and let it out in a little sigh. She wanted to hear the news herself, but her father nodded his head toward her. It was a clear suggestion for her to leave so the men could discuss the matter. What was the news, she wondered? As an obedient daughter, she closed the door quietly and went back to the front office.

J.D. Hackman did not linger. After a short time, he left her father's office, brushed past Louisa, and hurried out of the bank. She watched him as he walked down Main Street and out of sight. Then she walked briskly to her father's office, where he sat pouring over some papers in front of him. "What is it, Father?" she asked breathlessly. "Have the police located Roger? And what about the money?"

The lines on Jack Bradford's furrowed brow relaxed and he grinned at his daughter. "The news is good, Louisa. The authorities apprehended Roger in Florida. They believe he planned to hop a ship to South America and stay there until things cooled off up here. He's evidently done that before when he pulled off other jobs. Roger Evans, alias several other names, eluded the police for many years it seems. But they have him in custody now."

"I don't want to see Roger if he comes back here for his trial. It would remind me of what a foolish person I've been. I've learned a few lessons of late."

"No, he won't be brought back to Waterville. Our bank theft, though serious in our eyes, does not compare to some others he's pulled off. He's been jailed in Boston to await trial. His largest and most serious theft occurred at a large bank in that city."

"Did the police recover the money, Father? I know you've been concerned about the large amount stolen, especially since you had to borrow from Uncle Phillip."

"Roger still had most of the cash at the time of his arrest, but not all of it. Your Uncle Phillip has been patient and never asked for it once. But I want to get this debt paid back. It will lift a heavy load from my shoulders."

"Uncle Phillip has been a dear. He knows you will pay it back as soon as you are able. Did Mr. Hackman give you any idea when the money will be available?"

Jack Bradford removed his glasses and passed a hand over his eyes. A few strands of his neatly slicked brown hair had fallen across his forehead giving him a little boy look. "I must travel to Boston in another week for the trial. I'm one of the key witnesses in the investigation. It should be settled quickly due to the evidence and his past record. I will be able to settle my account with Phillip when I get back."

"Boston!" Louisa cried, as she smiled broadly and clapped her hands together. Then she whirled and twirled around the room while her full calico skirts billowed out around her. "I want to go with you, Father!"

Jack Bradford turned a perplexed gaze on his daughter. "Why, Louisa? You said you never wanted to see Roger Evans again. What made you change your mind?"

Louisa stopped her whirling and caught her breath. "I don't want to see Roger, Father. Ever again!"

"Then why are you excited about going to Boston, especially when I need you here."

Louisa's face grew serious as she eyed her father. She pushed back locks of gold hair and fastened the tresses with a silver clip. "There is someone I need to see. . .Annabelle Hayes. She lives in the outskirts of Boston. Peter gave me his cousin's address so I could write to him. I only wrote him one time, and it was an unkind letter. It led him to think I cared about someone else. Maybe Mrs. Hayes can give me some information about Peter."

"Wouldn't that be a little daring and forward, Louisa? It would seem you are pursuing the man. That isn't very lady-like. As I recall, it's the man who is to do the pursuing. . .not the woman!"

Louisa smiled mischievously at her father and he noticed the twinkle in her wide, gray eyes. She lifted one graceful hand and patted his cheek. "Fiddlesticks! I don't mind being the pursuer! If our relationship is broken, I'm the one who caused it, and I'm also the one to mend it, if possible. I'll not wait any longer for Peter to return to Waterville. If Annabelle Hayes is the kind of woman I think she is, she'll have some answers for me."

"What if they are not the answers you want, my dear?

Have you considered the alternative? Perhaps it will only add to your heartache. You can't toy with a man's affections and expect him to take it in stride. Men have their pride, you know. Peter McClough may have put you completely out of his mind. He may even have a new woman in his life."

Louisa's gray eyes filled with sparks of fire. "I'll fight for him, Father! I will! Peter loved me once! Maybe. . ." Her voice faltered and her lips trembled. "Maybe. . .Peter can find it in his heart to love me again."

eighteen

When Louisa and her father arrived home that afternoon, they shared Mr. Hackman's news with Elizabeth. She rejoiced with them about the capture of Roger Evans and recovery of most of the funds. Jack Bradford explained it necessitated a trip to Boston for the trial, but he said that with such clear evidence the matter should be settled quickly. Louisa proceeded to tell her mother she planned to accompany her father to Boston and explained her reasons.

"But Louisa, aren't you being a bit bold?" Elizabeth Bradford asked as she placed their meal on the dinner table. "You don't even know this Annabelle Hayes. She may not want anything to do with you. And I don't want you traveling around Boston alone while your father is at court."

"Mother, I'm not a child anymore. I'll be twenty-one soon. . .and a spinster at that. I don't need Father with me every moment!"

Jack Bradford coughed as he hid an amused smile and hastened to speak. "I'll go a day early, Elizabeth, and accompany our daughter to Mrs. Hayes' location. One short visit should take care of it. Don't worry, I won't let her traipse around town alone."

Elizabeth sighed with relief. "But, Jack, don't you need Louisa at the bank? Can your two employees carry on the workload without her help?"

"They've been with me a long while, Elizabeth, and proved themselves capable and trustworthy. I'm sure they will do fine. If a problem comes up, they can report to you. Remember, you worked with me some in the early years and have helped out from time to time. I don't see any

158

problem with the arrangement."

"Yes, I have some special memories of those times we shared together. I'll go down to the bank each morning and offer my help. It would be pleasant to work a few days at the bank again. It's a good place to meet people, and I always enjoyed talking to those who came in." Elizabeth fumbled with her apron pocket and pulled out an envelope. "Louisa, I almost forgot about the letter that arrived this afternoon."

A broad smile brightened Louisa's face as she eagerly reached for the envelope. "Is it from Peter, Mother? I've been looking for a letter from him."

"No, dear. It's from Emily out in Pennsylvania. Why don't you read it to us."

Louisa's brow furrowed. "I hoped Peter would write. Then I could get an idea how he feels about me now. . .and whether there is any hope for us." With a sigh she tore open the envelope. "But I do love to hear from Emily. I miss her so." She smoothed out the pale pink pages on the table before her and sniffed the delicate scent of lavender.

Dear Louisa,

I know I haven't written in a while, but things have been busy at the church. Our Christmas holidays were precious. . .just Robert and me in our own little home. We had some nice activities at the church. . .a special candlelight service on Christmas Eve along with songs by our little choir. I would enjoy singing with the choir, but they need me at the piano. It's fine because I enjoy that almost as well.

Have you heard any further word about Peter? I'm sure he was upset when he learned you were seeing someone else. My brother Frederic finally received a note from Tennessee, but Peter didn't go into detail about his situation. He sounded very mysterious and told Fred he wanted to discuss it in person when he got back. However, he gave no indication of when that would be, so it leaves us in the dark.

I do have some exciting news for you. No, I'm not expecting a baby. . .yet. We trust God will bless us with a child sometime soon, but it is all in His hands. My news is about Jim Bishop. He is the difficult man I told you about. It's so wonderful the way God works. This man, so bitter, so spiteful, so intent on causing chaos in the church, has repented of his sinful ways and recommitted his life to the Lord. What a joy it is to see him now! God worked a miracle in his life, and he is not the same man! It was the Christmas program and God's Holy Spirit working together. I told you he had to be disciplined by Robert and the deacons, and he had stopped coming to church. He allowed his children to be in the Christmas program, and his wife helped me with the production. Jim vowed he wouldn't come to see it or darken the church's door again. But he came in quietly at the last minute and took a seat at the back. The Christmas story, with the message of God's love, broke this man's heart. He's a huge hulk of a man, and I wish you could have seen him walk the aisle and kneel at the front. Tears streamed down his rugged cheeks as he made his peace with God. The rest of us joined him with tears of joy. What a glorious change! It's a complete turnaround. Now he is kind, considerate, and eager to help in any way he can. Robert has channeled Jim's energies in many directions. He's become a dedicated laborer for the Lord, and the Bishops are a happy family unit.

It was dreadful news about Roger Evans and the money your parents lost. We trust the authorities will locate him soon and bring him back to pay his debt to society. It is good you found out about his degenerate nature before you became more interested in this man. I can't imagine my dear friend married to such a person.

*I must close now and start preparation for our evening
meal. Please write soon and let me know the latest news*
Love, Your friend always,
Emily

"Isn't that good news about Jim Bishop?" Jack Bradford
asked. "One man with an embittered spirit can cause so much
stress in a local church. I'm thankful to know his attitudes
have changed, and he is now an asset to the church family. It
must be a great time of rejoicing for the Wampum Church."

"Yes, Father, Emily and Robert prayed about this concern
for a long time." Louisa gathered up some of the dishes and
carried them toward the kitchen. She paused at the doorway
and turned toward her parents, a smile stretched across her
wistful face. "And it's a real comfort to me. It tells me God
is still answering the prayers of His people."

ɛ

The next week Louisa and her father boarded the Kennebec
Railroad coach headed toward Boston, Massachusetts.
Louisa had mixed feelings about her venture, but it was too
late to turn back. While her father dozed or read the paper,
Louisa considered what Peter's reaction might be if he knew
she planned to confront his cousin. And how would Annabelle Hayes respond to her girlish outburst? She had committed to memory her plan of explanation and went over and
over the words in her mind. Would Mrs. Hayes consider her
fickle and childish? First she had cared for Peter, then she
didn't. Now she loved him again. It sounded very much like
a saga of discontent, and she had been discontented and, yes,
childish. But she had changed. The Louisa of yesterday no
longer existed. With God's help, she was stable and ready to
make a lifelong commitment to Peter. But what about Peter's
feelings? Would he believe the change in her was sincere or
would his manly pride stand in the way? Perhaps she had
shattered his love to a point of no return. A wistfulness

stretched across Louisa's face as she gazed out the window of the coach. The rolling hills and beauty of the countryside could not ease the pain in her heart. Her eyes lingered on the farms with their barns and outbuildings. The snow-covered stone fences stretched across the pastures were especially picturesque. And the little creeks, partly frozen, still bubbled along like a merry melody. She scolded herself and straightened the slumped shoulders. "God's creation is such a delight to behold," she whispered. "I'll feast my eyes upon His magnificent handiwork and allow only good thoughts to permeate my mind. Why despair over something I have no control over? I'll know soon enough where I stand. Peter's cousin may not have all the answers, but she can tell me if there is another woman in Peter's life."

When Jack Bradford awoke from a short nap, he found his daughter in a relaxed and cheerful mood. They talked quietly together, and Louisa pointed out the beauty of the countryside as the train whizzed past towns and rural areas. Once in Boston, Jack Bradford hired a sleigh to take them to their lodgings. He secured two rooms in town, close to the courthouse.

"Tomorrow is a free day, Louisa," her father said as they ate dinner at a small cafe that evening. "I'll hire the sleigh again, and we'll ride out to see Annabelle Hayes. I hope the woman will be home, although I really don't understand the reason you wish to see her. She may not have any more information about Peter than you do."

"Oh, she must, Father. She's family. And regardless, I'll feel much better after I talk with her. She can relieve my mind about the seriousness of Peter's business in Tennessee. And," she added thoughtfully, "she may have some insight regarding Peter's love life. . .which I hope includes me!"

Jack Bradford sighed heavily and shook his head. "I'm doing this for you, Louisa, because I love you. Just be prepared for the worst thing that could happen. You told Peter you were seeing someone else, so he might be involved with another woman. Then think about why it wouldn't be so bad, after all."

"But it would, Father! It would be very bad, and I would be shattered! Why are you saying these things?"

"Because I love you, as I said, and I don't want to see my daughter hurt any further. Just be prepared, dear. That's all I ask."

Louisa looked down at her plate and toyed with her food. "All right, Father," she said. Her eyes were moist, but she smiled bravely. "I'll be prepared for the worst, but I'll be praying for the best. . .God's best."

Jack Bradford grinned and covered her hand with his. "That's my girl!"

The following morning Jack Bradford rented a team of horses and sleigh from a nearby livery stable. Louisa and her father, bundled warmly against the cold air, headed out of town to find the little cottage of Annabelle Hayes. The keeper at the livery stable was able to clarify Louisa's directions and drew them a small map. "It's a fur piece," he said. "But you'll find her place all right."

The ride was invigorating with the chilly temperature and snow in the air. Louisa marveled at the beauty of the countryside with its large farms and outbuildings, stone fences, and small creeks. There were a few animals in the fields, but she envisioned the pastures full of cattle and horses during the warmer weather. For now, she decided, most of the livestock were kept inside the large barns. When they arrived at Annabelle's cottage, Jack Bradford noticed smoke curling upward from the small chimney. "She must be home, Louisa! I'm grateful for that. Hopefully, she'll invite us in for a hot cup of tea."

Louisa patted her cold cheeks with her warm gloved hands. "I feel so alive, Father! It must be the cold air. My cheeks feel like two cold apples."

Jack Bradford laughed as he helped his daughter out of the

sleigh and tethered the team to the hitching post. In answer to their knock, a short, somewhat rotund woman opened the door. She wiped her hands on her checkered apron and greeted them with a grin that stretched across her round cheeks. "Hello, folks," she said, glancing from one to the other. "What can I do for you?"

"Are you Annabelle Hayes?" Louisa asked rather timidly.

"That I am!" she said heartily with a merry little laugh that echoed on and on.

Jack Bradford extended his hand. "I'm Jack Bradford and this is my daughter, Louisa. We're from Waterville, Maine."

"Come in! Come in!" Annabelle exclaimed as she reached for each of their hands. "What a lovely surprise! I've heard so much about you from Peter."

Annabelle took their warm wraps and settled them into chairs near the fireplace. "I've got the kettle on for tea," she said jovially, "and we'll soon have you warmed up. It's a long ride from town in the cold."

Louisa glanced around the cozy, homey room and studied pictures on the walls. The cottage was neat and well kept with simple furnishings. Floors of wide plank, pine boards caught her eye and brightly colored hand-braided rugs were placed in various spots around the room. There were several boxes off to one side filled with miscellaneous memorabilia.

"Don't mind my packed boxes," Annabelle said as she motioned toward the boxes. "I'm planning to move soon." She went to the kitchen and retrieved the kettle boiling on the wood stove. Annabelle bubbled with enthusiasm and kept up a lively chatter as she served steaming cups of tea and small cakes. "What brings you to the Boston area?" she asked, dropping into a chair facing the couple. "Did you hope to find Peter?"

When Louisa hesitated, Jack Bradford spoke up and told Annabelle about his problem. "I need to be in Boston for a court case, Mrs. Hayes. An unfortunate incident happened with one of my employees, and it was necessary for me to make the trip. Louisa decided to come with me."

"I'm sorry about the problem with your employee, Mr. Bradford, but I am glad you and Louisa are able to visit. I'm happy for this opportunity to meet you."

"Mrs. Hayes. . . ," Louisa hesitated, then continued softly, "I've been rather bold coming here like this. I wanted to meet you and ask about Peter's welfare. I understand he is in Tennessee, but perhaps you could assure me that he is all right. He has been so secretive about his travels and when he would return to Waterville. I wondered if he had some serious illness or other cause for alarm."

Annabelle studied the young, uplifted face before answering. "No, Peter is not seriously ill or nigh unto death, Miss Bradford. He has been through a great trauma and difficult time in Tennessee, but it came out well. We are thankful for that. He does suffer pain from another source, however."

Louisa stood up and walked back and forth across the room twisting her handkerchief in her hands. "I see. Would this other pain have anything to do with me, Mrs. Hayes?"

"Please call me Annabelle, won't you? And I'd like to call you Louisa, if I may."

"Of course, Annabelle. I would like that."

"Peter's pain is indeed because of you, Louisa. When he received your letter saying you were seeing another man and seemed to care about him, he was heartbroken. He kept it to himself for a long while before he finally shared the information. Peter's had a difficult time dealing with your possible marriage to someone else. Has the marriage been consummated yet?"

"Definitely not!" Louisa cried. "I admit I was foolish Annabelle. . .and fickle. The young man who swept me off my feet is a notorious thief. He was my father's employee who stole a great deal of money from the bank. But I realized our relationship was a mistake before that incident occurred. His character lacked everything I deemed important in a man. At first it was all show and attentiveness. Then he revealed his real personality, which lacked integrity. How foolish I was to let Peter believe I cared for this man."

"Why didn't you write to Peter and tell him it was over, child?" Annabelle asked. "It would have eased the load he carried about his young shoulders."

"I wanted to, but I was afraid. I thought Peter's pride would stand in the way. And I lacked spiritual depth at the time. It was necessary to get my life right with God first, which I did recently. Do you think if I wrote him now, and apologized, he'd forgive me Annabelle?"

"I think there is nothing that boy would rather hear!" Annabelle smiled broadly as she retrieved their tea cups and carried them into the kitchen. "But now I'd like you and your father to do a favor for me. Would you take me over to my church in your sleigh? I have a message for Pastor O'Neil, and he is usually at the church every afternoon. I see the sun has come out, and it has stopped snowing. It's only a short distance from here, and I walk it often. However, a sleigh ride would be nice, and it will give you an opportunity to see more of the countryside. Would that be possible, Mr. Bradford?"

"Of course, Mrs. Hayes," Jack Bradford said as he stood to his feet. "It would be our pleasure. Louisa and I would enjoy seeing your church."

It only took a few minutes for the trio to don their warm wraps and head outside to the sleigh. Annabelle brought along a covered basket with some of her tea cakes for the pastor and his family. "We've been blessed with such a fine minister and his wife for many years," she said tucking warm blankets around the three of them. "Ours is a small church because we're such a rural area, but the sweet fellowship among the believers has been precious."

With directions from Annabelle, Jack Bradford snapped the reins and headed the team down the road toward their destination. The sunshine glistened like diamonds on the snow-covered fields and caused Louisa to cry out in delight. "I love the way the sun sparkles on the fences and trees, Annabelle! God's beauty and handiwork is all around us!"

"Mrs. Hayes, you mentioned you have plans to move," Jack Bradford said as they made an abrupt turn to the right at the corner. "Aren't you going to miss your church and the people here?"

"Yes, I will, Mr. Bradford. Very much. But it's time to make a change in my life, and I think it will be for the best. I'll tell you more about it later after we get back to my place. The church is just ahead on the right, and you can hitch the team along the front."

Jack Bradford pulled the team to a halt in front of a small, white church complete with steeple and bell. Nestled on a small knoll among a grove of trees, it made a picturesque setting with the countryside as a backdrop. Little puffs of smoke from the church's chimney curled upward toward the heavens. A small cemetery, complete with iron fence and gate, lay off to one side overlooking a valley with farmhouses and outbuildings beyond. The neat rows of tombstones stood like little sentinels, covered with the pure white snow.

"It's so lovely," Louisa sighed. "It looks like a beautiful painting by a famous artist. I think I shall have to touch it to be sure it's real."

Annabelle's merry little laugh echoed forth and reverberated across the valley. "Louisa, would you mind going into the church and telling Pastor O'Neil I'm here. You are so much spryer than I am."

Louisa threw off her blanket and jumped quickly down from the sleigh. "I'll be able to see if your charming little church is real, Annabelle. I hoped it would be possible to go inside."

Gingerly Louisa approached the heavy wooden door leading into the church. Once inside she blinked her eyes in the darkened building. The sun had been so bright outside it took her a moment to get her bearings. She glanced around the entryway and entered the main sanctuary. There were stained glass windows along each wall and rows of pews on each side of a center aisle. She could make out a platform at the front and started slowly toward it. Behind the platform a stained glass window caught her attention. Sun streamed through its multicolored panes in the shape of a cross. The display of various shades bouncing around the room was magnificent. She stared at the array of color and felt a strange sense of peace.

Partway down the aisle Louisa hesitated. She noticed a lone figure sat on the front pew with his head bowed. *What shall I do? I mustn't interrupt Pastor O'Neil when he is praying.* She hesitated and turned to go, but a board creaked noisily, and the man in the pew raised his head.

"Pastor O'Neil," she called. "I'm so sorry to disturb your prayer. Annabelle Hayes is outside, and she has a message for you."

The figure stood up and turned toward her. He pushed back a shock of dark hair which had fallen across his forehead. "Louisa!" he cried starting toward her. "Louisa, is that you. . .or am I dreaming?"

"Peter!" she shouted, running down the aisle toward him. "Oh, Peter, Annabelle didn't tell me you were here! She let me think you were off somewhere!"

Peter grabbed for her, and Louisa felt the strong arms surround her and draw her close. Her lips trembled as she lifted them to his. "Darling Louisa," he murmured huskily. "I thought. . .I thought. . .you had forgotten me."

Louisa's gray eyes searched his dark ones. "I couldn't forget you, Peter. I couldn't forget your boyish grin or the dark shock of hair that falls over your forehead. I couldn't forget how strong and brave you are. I've been a foolish, fickle girl. I was angry with you for going away and not sharing your reason with me or explaining how long you would be gone. In my despair, I drifted away from God and let myself be taken in by an unethical scoundrel. Can you ever forgive me? I've. . . I've never loved anyone but you."

Tenderly Peter traced the oval of her face with his finger and toyed with the golden ringlets curling along her cheek. Her body trembled at his touch as his dark eyes searched hers. "Those are the most beautiful words I've ever heard, darling," he said, kissing her tenderly on the lips. "Will you marry me soon, Miss Louisa Bradford, and make me the happiest man on God's earth?"

"Yes, Peter McClough. . .oh, yes!" Louisa said breathlessly, while tears gathered in the corners of her eyes and trickled down her cheeks.

"What's this? You're crying!"

"Tears of joy, Peter," she said as she smiled up at him. "They are only tears of happiness!" And straightaway he kissed her again!

epilogue

Roger Evans was brought to justice and jailed for his many crimes. The Bradford family regained most of the stolen money and repaid Jack's brother.

By God's grace, Peter's best laid plans finally materialized. The wedding took place the first Saturday in April in their Waterville church, with the present pastor and Rev. Robert Harris from Wampum, Pennsylvania, officiating. Louisa wore her mother's wedding gown and veil, all white satin and lace with fitted bodice and long train. Her hair, pulled back and secured with silver clips, allowed the golden tresses to cascade down her back. Her cousin Clara and good friend Emily, dressed in mint green satin with matching headpieces, stood with her.

Peter waited at the front in a black suit, the dark shock of hair slicked back from his forehead. Little muscles in both cheeks twitched from nervousness and excitement. Standing by him for support were his brother, Thomas, and best friend, Frederic Mason. Thomas, Genevieve, and Annabelle had arrived from Tennessee a day earlier to be there for the special occasion. A part of the honeymoon plans included a few days visiting Thomas and Genevieve at their plantation.

Peter felt God leading him to work with young boys. If agreeable with Thomas and Genevieve, Peter and Louisa would spend one or two months each summer at their estate in Tennessee conducting a Bible camp for boys. Along with Bible classes, the boys would learn responsibility. Part of their day would include various chores around the plantation such as gardening and care of the animals. There would be fun times and an opportunity to learn sportsmanship. Horseback riding, hiking, picnics, and campfires would be included. Louisa shared Peter's enthusiasm and dedication to such a ministry. God had done so much for the two of them, they considered it a privilege to invest time in training young lives for the Lord. The couple's deep love for one another was evident to all their friends and family as they repeated their vows of love and commitment. When the pastor presented them to the congregation as Mr. and Mrs. Peter McClough, Peter pulled Louisa's trembling body close and whispered huskily against the golden hair. "Darling, you are finally mine, and I'll never let you go!" Then he kissed her, long and tenderly, as her eyes once again filled with tears of joy.

A Letter To Our Readers

Dear Reader:

In order that we might better contribute to your reading enjoyment, we would appreciate your taking a few minutes to respond to the following questions. We welcome your comments and read each form and letter we receive. When completed, please return to the following:

Rebecca Germany, Fiction Editor
Heartsong Presents
PO Box 719
Uhrichsville, Ohio 44683

1. Did you enjoy reading *Best Laid Plans?*
   ❑ Very much. I would like to see more books
      by this author!
   ❑ Moderately
      I would have enjoyed it more if _____

   _____

   _____

2. Are you a member of **Heartsong Presents**? Yes ❑ No ❑
   If no, where did you purchase this book?_____

   _____

3. How would you rate, on a scale from 1 (poor) to 5 (superior), the cover design?_____

4. On a scale from 1 (poor) to 10 (superior), please rate the following elements.

   _____ Heroine   _____ Plot

   _____ Hero   _____ Inspirational theme

   _____ Setting   _____ Secondary characters

5. These characters were special because_____

_____

_____

6. How has this book inspired your life?_____

_____

_____

7. What settings would you like to see covered in future **Heartsong Presents** books?_____

_____

_____

8. What are some inspirational themes you would like to see treated in future books?_____

_____

_____

9. Would you be interested in reading other **Heartsong Presents** titles?   Yes ❑   No ❑

10. Please check your age range:
    ❑ Under 18   ❑ 18-24   ❑ 25-34
    ❑ 35-45   ❑ 46-55   ❑ Over 55

11. How many hours per week do you read?_____

Name _____

Occupation _____

Address _____

City _____ State _____ Zip _____

British COLUMBIA

The early twentieth century not only births the town of Dawson Creek, British Columbia, but changes it from a prairie village into the southern anchor of the Alcan Highway. Follow the fictionalized growth of author Janelle Burnham Schneider's hometown through the eyes of characters who hold onto hopes, dreams. . .and love.

This captivating volume combines four complete novels of inspiring love that you'll treasure.

paperback, 464 pages, 5 ³⁄₁₆" x 8"

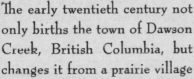

♥ ♥ ♥ ♥ ♥ ♥ ♥ ♥ ❤ ♥ ♥ ♥ ♥ ♥ ♥ ♥

♥ ♥ ♥ ♥ ♥ ♥ ♥ ♥ ❤ ♥ ♥ ♥ ♥ ♥ ♥ ♥